DIRT LULLABIES

JEREMY MEGARGEE

DIRT LULLABIES SECOND EDITION

ISBN-13: 978-1505853193

ISBN-10: 1505853192

www.facebook.com/JMHorrorFiction

For my family and my friends. For everyone who believed in me and supported me along the way. Thank you for helping to make my dream a reality.

"The oldest and strongest emotion of mankind is fear, and the oldest and strongest kind of fear is fear of the unknown."
- H. P. Lovecraft

Part I: Beneath

Chapter 1

Roman

I guess it all started with a promise.

A sweet whisper, seductive and full of possibilities.

I never should have listened. The trajectory of my life would have been very different if I had simply toned it out and ignored it. Pass it off on a vivid imagination and my own sense of morbid curiosity.

I could have let it fall on deaf ears. I could have crawled back out of that dark, musty root cellar and let the hard November rain fall upon my face and wash away any thoughts of what might be lurking beneath. That would have been the sensible thing to do...

But I didn't do that. I couldn't do that. It was like invisible serpents twisting and twirling from that hole in the earth, embracing me, pulling me close...cupping my chin and flitting forked tongues against my naive ears. Willpower wasn't an option. Turning my back on the promise seemed akin to shutting the ancient stone doors of something so valuable, so precious...a once in a lifetime opportunity.

It spoke to me of things unknowable, a bitter breath coming from that cracked and forgotten place beneath my old house in rural West Virginia. I still remember the scent of it curling into my nostrils. The stink of sour soil...and beneath that? Something older. Something stranger. Something worse.

I didn't comprehend the lies spewing up from that dark place. At that time I didn't even realize they were lies. I didn't understand the *nature* of what lived down there. I knew only that the promise seemed like my salvation...and the salvation of my family.

For me...what came out of that hole was hope.

But I'm getting ahead of myself, aren't I?

Every story should have a beginning.

My name is Roman Merrick.

And this story is mine.

Chapter 2

Roman

We never starved, that's the important thing to remember. Regardless though, life was tough. It was a meager paycheck to paycheck existence. My mother never graduated high school and suffered from dystonia so she wasn't able to work. My father was a determined man, but his ambitions never rose beyond manual labor. He labored long and difficult hours to keep food on the table, rather it be via the pushing of a lawnmower or the swirling of a mop on a dirty barroom floor.

To be perfectly honest, we were pretty damn poor. We took what joy we could from the companionship of one another and we drew our strength from the bond of a tight-knit family. We struggled daily...sometimes we stumbled and faltered...but it was our shared strength that kept us from falling for good.

I was born into this kind of lifestyle and rather than attempt to rise above it, I allowed myself to settle into the grim reality of it all. I came to accept that my future would be very similar to that of my father's future. There was no shame in that for me.

Mine is a soul that soars when lost in fiction, so rather than set out on a path of higher education...I chose to pour myself into every thick book the library could offer me. I read because I enjoyed reading. To me, opening the binding of a book was like opening a door to entirely different worlds.

My library card was the key to these mysterious doors and in many ways it empowered me, made me feel like a gatekeeper with access to places few ever get the chance to visit.

Best of all? It was free.

I'd lived most of my childhood on the edge of desolation, tipping dangerously close towards the abyss of life on the streets and the loss of a roof atop my head, so when granted the promise of an escape? Rather it be via mythical odysseys or modern tales of terror...I was eager to capture that.

I realize now that it's been a theme in my life.

Promises.

The promises held in books, sometimes the pages crisp and new, other times yellowed and dusty...offering you a wealth of knowledge. The seductive pull takes hold and you just let yourself become lost. You like how it feels...you let the stories carry you away.

I loved books.

I loved my family.

I was content.

But even so...the bills were piling up. The calls from the debt collectors were coming more and more frequently. New lines of worry furrowed my father's brow...and a terrible sense of escalation glimmered in my mother's eyes whenever I met them with my own.

We'd stumbled before, but always managed to catch ourselves before it was too late. This time was different. I could feel it in my bones. The beast of destitution was close, gnawing and slavering at the walls...threatening to leave nothing but ragged ruin at my family's feet.

Dark times looming.

Bad days coming.

We needed a paying promise now more than ever before.

Chapter 3

Roman

I was in my early twenties then. I worked at a local cemetery, mostly doing landscaping. It was seasonal work and the season was winding down as the cold weather became more prevalent. Gone were the days of summer when I'd navigate an aging push mower around lines of tombstones, my battered secondhand iPod strapped to my hip and some melodic rock blazing through my ears.

Those moments were peaceful. The tombstones were like a maze that I was exploring, the mower engine churning and the thrum of it felt through my fingertips as I moved onward and onward. There was no real destination, no purpose to the maze. Just the tranquility of the exploration was enough for me.

Sometimes I'd stop and read the names on the stones or wonder about the dates. I think the oldest headstones interested me the most, the ones so worn and eroded that nothing was left to memorialize the person that dwelled in the box below. Those made me a little sad too.

All things fade with time...and headstones are a perfect example of this. The years go on and on and the past is pushed deeper and deeper into the shadows. I thought about who these people were, the things they did in life...the legacies they left behind. Did they have families? Or were they just lonely footnotes planted into the earth and then forgotten?

That's the mystique of the cemetery and these old stones.

I enjoyed the mystique much more than I enjoyed the minimum wage pay. I usually worked late evenings, my little tin lunch pail resting on a stone as the sun slowly faded on the horizon. There was some rusty fencing on the edge of the cemetery and beyond that a thick pine forest...and the sun always set behind that forest, painting the pines with reddish vibrancy, setting the forest ablaze with color.

I'd eat my bologna and cheese sandwich and think during times like this. I'd twist and turn ideas around in my mind...struggling to come up with a solution to the financial situation my family and I found ourselves in. I'm a dreamer at heart and most of my ideas seemed too broad, too ambitious...not concrete enough to yield actual results.

When you're dirt poor and rock bottom is dangerously close...you start to realize why criminals resort to certain choices out of pure desperation. It doesn't matter if it's to feed addictions or to feed a growing family, sometimes the taboo path seems like the easiest shortcut.

Should I turn to thievery?

Nah. The consequences far outweighed the reward if something went wrong. Plus I don't think I'd be a very successful bank robber. Those kind of jobs require teamwork and collusion...and I'd always been kind of a loner.

Twilight was approaching and I was barely fifteen minutes away from getting off work when I must have just dozed off. I was lying back on one of the large tombstones, my lunch pail beside me. I'd heard that it's disrespectful to walk across or linger on a tombstone...but I never looked at it that way.

I always figured the dead would appreciate all the company they could get.

I awoke, or thought I awoke...but everything was wrong.

The stars seemed too close, like bright little pinpricks in the sea of darkness that was the sky. The moon was leering and bone-colored...close enough to reach out and touch. A bitter wind traveled around me, dead leaves swirling and swirling and never seeming to touch the ground, almost like they were caught in slow motion.

That's when I noticed the old man in the filthy brown suit.

It had been black once but the soil of his grave had ruined that, giving it a mottled and dirt-encrusted veneer. Most of his face was draped in shadow...and I'm thankful for that. All that I could see was his mouth, the flesh of his lips rotten and black, his teeth seeming too long thanks to the receding gum line.

He was speaking, whispering...but I heard nothing.

Finally I saw his hand moving downward, a bony finger pointing. I marveled in horror at the maggots wriggling and dropping from the sleeve of his suit to hit the ground in mesmerizing slow motion.

He was pointing at one of those old, worn stones...the ones I found so interesting.

New words had formed on this stone, etched fresh and ragged, as though the old man had dug them in recently with what remained of his broken fingernails.

"DO NOT LISTEN TO IT."

"DO NOT FEED IT."

"BURY IT DEEPER AND SALT THE EARTH."

"IF YOU LET IT SPEAK...IT WILL BE YOUR RUIN."

I was trying to comprehend this when the old man's mouth stretched open, wider and wider, the jaw seeming to come unhinged as bits of tattered flesh fell to the ground. I heard him then. I heard him scream...the sound mixing in with something like the buzzing of a thousand flies.

And then I awoke for real.

Chapter 4

Roman

The dream stayed with me throughout the night. Even after I got home and watched some television, my mind couldn't focus on any of the flashing images on the screen. I kept seeing the hollow curve of the old man's mouth, the maggots falling from his sleeve...and the message scrawled on that tombstone.

A warning?

A threat?

I didn't know. I'd had vivid dreams before, but this one seemed somehow pivotal...like I remembered every detail of it because I was *supposed* to. Just when my mind didn't need anymore to weigh it down, entirely new and unpleasant thoughts have entered into the playing field like vultures circling carrion.

Even when I tried to follow the threads of the dream it just gave birth to entirely new questions.

Who shouldn't I listen to? Who shouldn't I feed? Bury it deep and salt the earth...none of it made any sense. And maybe that's the point. Dreams aren't necessarily supposed to make sense. They're just a cosmic bowl of colorful soup regurgitated from the subconscious, full of random images and half-formed concepts. I shouldn't obsess on a dream. It's fruitless and pointless and it gets me nowhere.

I tried to just shut it out and forget about it. I found myself wandering out to the cracked, sagging porch steps beyond the threshold of the back door. I sat there and let the cold sink into my bones a bit. I lit up a cigarette, inhaling deeply, the tendrils of smoke curling up into the night air.

The bulb that once illuminated the porch had burnt out and nobody had replaced it yet, so the only light to be found was the burning ember of my cigarette. Weak light...especially when up against a darkness as strong as a moonless night in the countryside.

Something stirred in the bushes beyond the steps. Something was watching me. I couldn't make out any sort of form in the shadows, but I felt it regardless.

It was getting closer, the dead leaves crunching underfoot.

I could see it now emerging from the gloom, staring at me with bright, attentive eyes. A little stray kitten. One of many that called my yard home, a litter of four lived beneath a ratty overturned couch near the side of the house if memory served. This one was all white with a touch of black along the nose, and probably the most curious one of the bunch.

I reached down to stroke it behind the ears and it responded to my touch with a warm little purr, so throaty and reassuring.

Few sounds in this world are as pleasant as the sound of a content cat purring for affection. It's a little joy...but one worth savoring.

So I smoked and I gave the little cat all the affection that it craved, making sure to rub its little white belly as it rolled happily across the blanket of dead leaves on the ground.

I let all thoughts of the dream fade.

And fade they did, although reluctantly.

Chapter 5

Roman

It had been about a week since that night in the cemetery. It wasn't fresh in my mind anymore and once you get into the routine of everyday life, even something as bizarre as that dream starts to drift out of your thoughts. I was concerned with more pressing problems.

My father was driving me down the same back road we'd taken for years to get into town. I knew every field, every house and seemingly every tree along the way. Even the cows looked familiar, their breath pluming out past lolling tongues. It was a quiet drive and I found myself studying the remnants of a man-made rock wall at the edge of a cornfield.

The corn stalks were long dead, brown and lifeless, the wind tearing through them mercilessly. The heater in the family Buick wasn't much competition for wind like that, and even though all the windows were wound up a few gusts of that sharp cold still managed to seep into the car with us.

We were bundled up tight, my father in his favorite denim jacket and a Marlboro hat pulled down low across his face. His black eyes, studious and observant as ever, were focused solely on the asphalt ahead of him.

Braham Merrick never spoke much. One might call him the strong silent type, and it seemed that I'd inherited that same mindset from my dad. We spoke when we had something worth saying, and every word was chosen carefully.

The silences between us occurred often...but they were comfortable silences. We understood each other. We never bothered with meaningless small talk simply for the sake of it.

So on the rare occasions when my father does speak I make it a point to listen.

"Electric bill is past due. We're on the payment plan...but we still owe on last month's bill too. I'm trying to make it work, son...but it's getting harder and harder."

I'd overheard my folks talking about this before but I feigned surprise.

"We'll figure it out, dad. We always do. We'll sell something, or maybe I can pick up a few more shifts..."

Braham nodded, his hands tightening on the steering wheel, but the sigh that escaped his mouth sounded so bleak, the effect heightened by the fog of the cold air expelling past his bearded lips. It hurt me seeing him like that. A proud, hard working man...reduced to making that kind of sound.

"I'm not gonna lie to you, Roman. We're in it pretty deep this time. Car insurance is about to lapse. I just...don't have the money to keep up with it anymore. We barely covered rent this month, and I got no idea what we're gonna be able to do for next month. There ain't much left to sell, son..."

He pauses, a calloused hand scrubbing against one gray, scruff-covered cheek.

"What little I'm making at the American Legion helps, but mopping floors and scrubbing tables don't necessarily lead you to a life of fame and fortune. And your job is winding down...warm weather ain't nothing but a memory now. Supposed to be even colder next month..."

I struggled to find a glimmer of light in a dark situation.

"They might keep me on a bit longer to clean up old floral arrangements and help with grave digging. I'll find another job soon..."

Dad looked at me out the corner of his eye, the brakes screeching and crying a bit as we rounded an especially sharp corner. The pads needed to be replaced, but who has the money for that?

"It's gonna be a scrape...but we've scraped before. We always come out on the other side of it. Everything we been through, seems we're due for some good luck pretty damn soon, don't it?"

He smiles. Even though he's never been to a dentist a day in his life, my dad's teeth are practically perfect. I've always been amazed by that.

I smile back and I'm seconds away from replying when the front passenger tire blows out. There's the sound of dragging tread and the smell of burnt rubber as my father struggles to guide the Buick over onto the road's shoulder.

We just sit there for a moment, saying nothing.

When fate seems intent on fucking you in every conceivable way on the worst possible days...

There just isn't much to say.

Chapter 6

Roman

Two days later I lost my job, as my father predicted. I received my last paycheck from the grizzled cemetery owner as he watched reruns of Tales from the Crypt on the little TV in his back office while simultaneously shoving generic potato chips into his mouth.

I asked him about the possibility of keeping me on into the winter months for general maintenance around the grounds, little odd jobs and things like that. His response was a perfect representation of the kind of man he was.

"Ain't nuttin to do with the dead in winter except let em freeze right along with everything else. Can't save wilting flowers and ain't no work to be done after November. See ya next spring, kiddo."

He knew I was facing hardships. He just didn't give a shit...

At this point in my life unemployment was the last thing I needed, but regardless of what I needed...

It's what I got.

Chapter 7

Roman

There weren't many jobs in Rust Valley, West Virginia. The gradual economic decline certainly hadn't helped matters, but even when the economy was stable this town never really offered a great deal of options. Most of the steady work came from the few remaining coal mines and Strickland Steel, the only steel mill for miles around.

I couldn't let that dissuade me though. I went from shop to restaurant, filling out as many physical applications as I possibly could. I'd heard the coal mines weren't hiring right now so that possibility was already off the table. I made a special trip out to Strickland and spoke to the foreman there, and he promised to keep my name in the running if one of the entry level positions opened up.

It wasn't the search that was hard. If anything I enjoyed the search, it kept me busy, made me feel like I was contributing in some very basic way. It was the waiting game that killed me. When you're without steady work all the power relies solely in the hands of the employer...and sometimes it feels like they're dangling you over the rushing current of a river, and you never know if they're gonna drop you in to drown or pull you back up to safety.

It's that *not* knowing that makes the process so damn frustrating.

I spent hours in the library just banging out online applications until my fingers were sore from typing. This wasn't a question of finding some part-time job so that I'd have spending money for video games or new clothes or whatever...

This was a question of survival.

I needed to do everything I possibly could to keep my head above water. I could feel the pressure closing in on me from all sides, the image of my little family flashing across my mind every time I filled out a new application or spoke to a new uncaring manager about the possibility of finding work.

The lights, the heat, the water, the phone, the car, the food...

It all kept adding up, it all kept eating at me.

I had to do my part to fix this before it veered off into the realm of the unfixable.

My mother had given me one of her prized possessions earlier that day. It was a diamond ring with the tiniest black flaw in the middle. A family heirloom that had come down the bloodline from her great-grandmother, something mom cherished. It broke something in me seeing her give that up. A little fragment of my soul, shattered shrapnel that seemed to grind against my emotions.

But I knew what we were up against, so I took that ring and got into the Buick, a temporary hard tire replacing the one that had blown out a few days ago. I drove to that grimy pawnshop; I went to that sleazy pawnbroker while swallowing my pride but still determined to not be swindled.

Mom's sacrifice would buy us some time, and time was something we desperately needed right now.

He had his jeweler take a look at it and I was just about to start haggling price when the ring was placed back into my hand, the pawnbroker already turning away.

They had no interest in it.

The diamond was a fake.

Chapter 8

Roman

I got home late that night, the headlights blaring across the barren dirt driveway leading back to the house. We lived in the middle of nowhere, a few mobile homes lining the road at random intervals, some occupied, some simply abandoned. Ours was the only actual "house" in the neighborhood (if you'd even want to call it that) It was a mutt in every sense of the word. It had been cobbled together and remodeled time and time again, styles clashing and ramshackle partitions added on over the years by previous owners.

It was like a house that had no idea what it wanted to be, hadn't really discovered its identity yet. The last rebuild had been sometime in the early 1970s according to the landlord. He also told us that there had been many houses on the property long before that, some of them torn down, others burnt down...and they were just rebuilt over the old foundations over and over again.

Sometimes half-charred walls or crumbling chimneys were even recycled and incorporated into the rebuild, the most striking example of this a random chimney that juts out from the wall of my bedroom despite the fact that there's no fireplace to be found in the home. Not anymore, at least...

It was outfitted with baseboard heat, but it seemed like the old heaters malfunctioned or didn't work properly at all because the house was always freezing from late November straight through the winter months.

I wasn't looking forward to returning home empty-handed, the ring shoved down into my front pocket. I considered lying about why the pawnbroker wouldn't bite, but what could I say? The emotional value my mother had invested into this ring was priceless. I couldn't even fathom trying to tell her that it was worthless; it seemed a conversation I just didn't have the heart or the energy for right now.

I decided I'd try to stall. I'd tell her that particular pawn shop was closed today and we'll have to try again another time. Maybe in the meantime I'd find the mental strength to sit down with her, look her in the eyes...and tell her the truth about the "diamond" that had been passed down through generation after generation of Harlans on her side of the family.

Maybe I'd even manage to do it without my voice croaking.

I pulled up in front of the house and killed the engine, taking a moment just to sit in the car and decompress a bit. I wound down the window, letting the wind lash at me as a lit up a fresh cigarette.

I felt suddenly very tired, exhausted even.

I don't know why...but I started thinking about that dream again. The corpse in the dirty brown suit. The decaying mouth that spoke nothingness. That tombstone marked with riddles.

I shook my head and flicked the cigarette out the window, pausing to open up the car door and then slam it shut again.

I headed towards the front door with my hands shoved down deep into the pockets of my jeans, my head hanging low against the wind.

I wasn't in the mood for haunts tonight.

Chapter 9

Roman

Helena Merrick was the kindest mom a guy could ever ask for. She went above and beyond to give me the best childhood possible despite our less than fortunate situation. There were moments I remember when food was scarce, but there was a never a moment when I went to bed with hunger pangs in my gut.

She did what was necessary to ensure the health and well-being of her family. Sometimes it was seeking out government assistance or taking a trip down to the local food bank, she bit back her pride in exchange for the ability to provide.

Just like dad she had worked hard since she was a young girl, but dystonia hit her fairly early in life and limited her mobility considerably. She took various medications to combat the disorder but the involuntary muscle spasms still tormented her, usually in the form of her head tilting uncontrollably to the left for seemingly no reason at all.

The disorder pained her but it never broke her. The Harlan side of the family has deep roots in the oldest parts of West Virginia, and almost all of the family members are known for rawboned toughness. My mother was no different.

I sat with her in the little living room, struggling to find the right words to describe how the day had went. I tried to sound optimistic about the job hunt.

She listened quietly, those minute muscle contractions coming at steady intervals but never impacting her concentration.

Even approaching her golden years, Helena had beautiful features, a face with heart-like curves. The wrinkles only added more character to her expressions, more depth to the warmth of her smile. Her eyes were the palest green, catlike and hypnotizing. My eyes are the same shade, only a bit darker on the spectrum.

"How about Strickland? They taking anyone on?"

She seemed mildly curious when she asked this, trying to hide the hopeful lilt in her voice and doing a pretty good job of it.

I almost didn't even notice.

I could only shake my head in uncertainty, my hands clasped between my knees.

"They said they'd keep me in mind. You know the turnover rate is high down there. There's a pretty good chance something might open up soon...just a matter of time."

I think I did a decent job of sounding hopeful too. I flashed a smile to drive away the dispirited feeling in my heart, and it seemed to satisfy her, or at least charm her enough to move away from the topic.

"And the ring? Fetch a good price?"

I'd managed to skirt that topic too up to this point. The little white lie about the pawn shop being closed was already forming on my lips, seconds away from being articulated by my tongue.

But before I could even begin to reply...

Every light in the house snapped off all at once.

Chapter 10

Roman

I held tight to the brief hope that maybe someone had hit an electric pole somewhere down the lane. I tried convincing myself that maybe there was a problem with the breaker box or something like that. But deep down inside I knew the cold, hollow truth.

My mother's words served only to solidify that truth.

"Those bastards...I told them we'd pay them when we could..."

She trailed off and I could just make out her darkened form, already starting to shiver a bit as the heat slowly dissipated from the house.

"This is wrong what they're doing to us. Parasites trying to suck us dry, don't they understand that?? I told Braham they'd do it, he didn't believe me...not when it's this cold out, but..."

She started stammering, the frustration robbing her of words.

I sat down next to her, my arm stretching across her shoulders to give her what little comfort I could. There was a woolen blanket stretched across the back of the couch and I paused only to unfurl it and wrap it around Helena's shoulders. She pulled it close around her throat like a shawl, her fingers trembling.

We'd been up against it before. Even as a kid growing up I remember seeing the occasional disconnect notice lying on the kitchen table. I remembered overhearing desperate, hushed conversations after I'd gone to bed at night. We lived in another part of town then, a little apartment where the walls were thin and voices carried.

I'd lie there staring at the ceiling with a tattered Goosebumps book cradled to my frail chest, listening to Helena and Braham exchanging ideas on exactly how they'd manage to pay the electric bill that month.

Sometimes they'd have to borrow from extended family or work extra shifts but in the long run the bill always got paid. It was like watching them on a teeter-totter struggling to keep on the side of stability and avoiding the impoverished darkness waiting on the other side. I was just a kid then...and it made me feel so helpless.

This was the first time in all of those years of struggle that the utility company actually shut the power off for nonpayment though. Somehow it made it feel more *real*. It opened my eyes to just how bad our situation was becoming, that gradual slide into destitution seeming to pick up speed at such an alarming rate.

I found a flashlight in one of the bureau drawers, had to smack my hand against it a few times to keep the illumination from flickering off. The batteries hadn't been replaced in a long time.

I shined it towards Helena, keeping the light lowered to avoid shining it in her eyes. She was wringing her hands together in her lap, her shallow breathing seeming especially loud now that the house was totally silent and devoid of all the white noise of household appliances.

"Do we have candles?"

"Not up here. I remember seeing an old box down in the root cellar when we first moved in though. I don't even know if the wicks are still usable, son..."

We never went down into that root cellar. It was a dank, ruined old place and there was just no reason to go down there. We'd lived in this house for years now and the only time I can remember even seeing it was during the brief tour the landlord took us on when we were still considering renting the place.

And even then I only got the smallest glimpse of the interior. Small, cramped. A floor composed of dirt and dust-coated cobwebs hanging from the termite-eaten support beams. There were a few old boxes down there left over from previous owners.

"It's better than nothing."

I took time to pull on my heavy black overcoat, my grip on the flashlight tightening.

"We'll get through this, mom. Just try and stay warm...be back in a minute."

I offered my mom what I hoped was a reassuring smile before exiting through the side door of the house. The wind greeted me with icy kisses and I was less than thrilled to see that a light, steady rain had started falling from the starless sky.

A few droplets caught in my eyelashes as I started off towards the root cellar.

I blinked them away.

They felt like frigid tears oozing down my cheeks.

Chapter 11

Roman

The only entrance to the root cellar is near the back of the house. It's surrounded by a swampy little area overgrown by all manner of invasive plant life. Ivy creeps along the outer walls, gnarled willow trees loom overhead, their limbs hanging downward like deformed hands with terribly long bark-encrusted fingers. It's dark and shady even on the sunniest of days and moss covers the aging concrete blocks that lead down to the door.

Little streams of groundwater travel down from farther up the hill and all of the runoff leads to the swampy section of earth, feeding into it and giving rise to the vegetation. Just getting to the door is like venturing into a claustrophobic maze of branches and shrubbery and I have to struggle to keep the sharp edges from reaching out and tearing lacerations into my face.

It's even harder on a night this black and cold, my only solace coming from the weak beam of a flashlight that might not last much longer.

The door is small, child-sized. The wood is rotten and mildewed and the hinges so rusty that when I open it a few flaky screws simply fall to the dirt floor.

I'm over six feet so I have to bend way down to pass through the threshold, my shoulders stooped and my neck craned forward. I felt the sticky, nasty sensation of cobwebs collecting in my hair. It was so musty down here, no fresh air to be found, only the scent of soil and some cloying odor that I couldn't really identify.

My eyes began to water a bit and I had to swallow back some of the saliva that had collected in my throat just to avoid choking on it.

The root cellar was fairly barren, an extremely small place. I swept the flashlight from side to side, the flickering light taking in the confines. The floor was hardened dirt, a few broken cobblestones here and there where someone must have tried to cover it but never finished the job.

The walls were comprised of old, moldy wood. A few support beams jutted out from the earth here and there. The few boxes that remained down here were piled up in one corner.

I became aware of an intensely cold draft coming from somewhere, even colder than the air outside...but I couldn't detect where exactly it was coming from.

I headed towards the boxes, reaching out with the tip of the flashlight and pushing back the crumbling cardboard lids. I had noticed a few old snake skins hanging from some ragged holes in the cellar's low ceiling so I was wary about my exploration of the boxes. The last thing I needed right now was to open up a box and have a serpent spring forth and sink needle fangs into my flesh...

Some of the boxes were empty, some contained broken nicknacks. Finally I came across the one I was looking for. A box filled with fat, stubby candles. The wax was an ugly yellowish color, but they looked like they'd light up okay.

I wedged the flashlight into the crook of my elbow and took the box up into my arms, doing my best to get it well positioned against my chest.

I was halfway across the cellar when I felt something crawling across my hand. My breath caught in my throat, my eyes started to drift slowly downward. I tilted the flashlight up as much as I could while still maintaining my hold on the box...

The weak, faltering light caught on hideous little black eyes and numerous spindly legs walking across the flesh of my hand.

A loud "FUCKKKKK" roared from my lips at the sight of the house centipede, and I whipped my hand to the side to dislodge it, losing my grip on the box in the process. The centipede flew off and hit the wall as the candles tumbled down against the floor, rolling every which way.

I took a moment to compose myself, pausing only to scrub at my hand to try and drive away the very sensation of all those legs crawling on me.

Finally I dropped down to my knees on the dirt floor and began to collect the candles one by one, placing them back into the box. I got closer to the middle of the root cellar's floor...and found something puzzling. Something I hadn't noticed before when I came in.

It was the source of that cold draft.

There was a jagged crack in the earth here, maybe a few inches across on each side. The air that came up out of it was freezing, seeming to dry out my nostrils the very second I held my head overtop it.

I shined the beam of the flashlight down into the crack but could make nothing out but earthy walls descending deeper and an abyss of impenetrable blackness. There was nothing to be seen, nothing the light could penetrate at least.

That's when I noticed the smell. I struggle to find words that might do justice to that smell. It was an overpowering sweetness, like meat gone rotten and left out in the sun for a very long time. It mingled with the scent of dirt, something long buried and long forgotten. It was unlike anything I'd ever experienced before...

I was trying to understand what I was seeing. As far as I knew there was nothing below the root cellar. No subbasement, no deeper part of the house.

The floor here was dirt...and there was nothing down there but more dirt.

The light still shined in my hand, the weak rays casting the slightest glow across the crack. I was still trying to wrap my head around the mysterious hole when I heard something down there.

My blood seemed to momentarily freeze in my veins and all the breath expelled from my lungs so quickly that I forgot to draw new oxygen back in.

It was the sound of something shifting down in the deep. Some enormous, unknowable weight. It was followed by a muddled, murky sound.

Something like an animal waking from a slumber.

I'd heard enough.

I finally managed to *tear* a few new breaths into my body and I scrambled to my feet, the candles all but forgotten. I half-ran and half-stumbled towards the door, my only goal at that particular moment in time to get away as quickly as humanly possible.

Something stopped me with my hand on the door.

A voice floating up from that hole in the dirt.

The first time I heard it I could not ascertain any kind of gender for the thing that lived below. It was both throaty and masculine and silky and feminine all at the same time. Perfectly androgynous...and perfectly charming.

It froze me in place, the hair standing up on the back of my head and goosebumps breaking out along the flesh of my arms.

This was something new for me. A terror so profound that I could not even summon the strength to move. As I stood there, petrified and motionless, I could sympathize with a deer caught in the headlights. I understood why the rabbit froze while staring down the wolf.

In final, precious moments like these...every part of you shuts down and waits. You wait in motionless silence for life to return or death to take you. You wait...and the waiting is the worst part.

The words that voice spoke throbbed in my head just as much as they rang in my ears. I seemed to hear it in every single nerve ending inside of my body.

"Don't go."

Chapter 12

Roman

I felt my head slowing craning around to look over my shoulder. The root cellar remained unchanged, the crack in the earth looking more ominous than ever. For a moment the fear took a backseat to self-doubt. Did I just imagine that voice? Did I have an auditory hallucination or something?

Was I losing my fuckin' mind?

The silence seems to stretch on for a bit and reinforce this theory. I'm about to turn away again when the theory shatters into a million pieces and the fear returns, blazing back into my heart like a persistent locomotive.

"Don't be afraid. Madness isn't to blame..."

A pause, and then the voice comes again, seeming to echo up out of that hole.

"I am speaking to you."

I'm at a loss. My heart is hammering and it feels like I haven't blinked in almost five minutes straight. I'm horrified about what might happen if I close my eyes even for a split second.

"I'd imagine it's a bit shocking. I'm a little surprised myself. Haven't had a visitor in a very long time. Gets lonely..."

A voice from a hole in the ground is attempting to have a conversation with me. This is actually happening. My hand reaches up, shaking a bit...to pinch my cheek. If this is a nightmare...the pinch does nothing to wake me up.

"Forgive me. I'm sleepy. You woke me up...not much room to stretch down here."

The conversation is a bit one-sided and I'm starting to fear that if I don't respond to the thing soon that it might make matters even worse. I open my mouth to speak but no actual words come out. At best I manage a sound like the belligerent moan of a village idiot...

"Uhhhrr..."

It's answered almost immediately.

"Mmm. Fascinating. Not a big talker, huh?"

I'm momentarily disarmed and the fear fades a little, taking a backseat to a sense of overwhelming curiosity. When I speak again I'm able to do so a bit more coherently.

"What...who are you?"

"That's complicated."

In spite of myself I'm walking back towards the crack, almost like I'm drawn to it.

"Do...you have a name?"

"Humans...gotta love em'. Always have to put labels on things. Names. Words. Letters. Now I know my ABCs, next time won't you sing with me!"

The voice is strangely melodic and before I even realize it I'm sitting down cross-legged in front of that hole, the flashlight held in my lap. I clicked it off. I'm not sure if the voice appreciates light...

"Z...too zany. B...too boring. M...that's a good, strong letter."

My eyes are wide, my mouth hanging open.

"Call me M."

"Okay. M..." I respond slowly, my voice still shaky.

"And you are...don't tell me! Roman, right?"

My mouth feels terribly dry. I try to wet my lips but it doesn't do much good.

"How do you know my name?"

"I know lots of things. I'm a knower, Roman. An eater of knowledge, you might say. I pick things up here and there. Got quite the intuitive streak in me..."

I'm trying to think of what I should ask next. I have thousands of questions and each one sounds more ridiculous in my head than the last. Before I can even attempt to formulate a new question, M speaks again.

"For example, I know you've fallen on hard times. I know that it's lights out up there in the Merrick household right now. Just the thought makes me chilly...no fun!"

"Yeah...we don't have the money to pay the bill right now. It's rough."

A pause, and then that strange sound from earlier, like tremendous weight shifting somewhere below.

"Life is rough, pal. Doesn't have to be, though. I can help."

My eyebrows arch quizzically.

"See that rusty old toolbox in the corner there? Kinda hidden, camouflaged by dust. Take a peek inside. You might find a helping hand."

A part of me is reluctant to move because all of this still seems so surreal. I try to push that part of me to the side as I reach for the toolbox. I never would have even seen it if not for M pointing it out. It's practically buried in dust and splinters of wood.

I swallow deeply and then open it, the hinges creaking.

There are old wrenches inside, a few rust-speckled bolts and screws, but overtop it all is a thin stack of bills bound with a tattered rubber band.

I take the cash into my hand, marveling at it for a moment. There are ten hundred dollar bills in the bundle, all of them bearing dates from the late 1960s.

I turn to the hole, a smile breaking across my mouth before I know it's even there.

"Is this money yours?"

There's a sound from the depths of the dirt. It's like the jangling of a music box buried in the very center of the earth. It takes me a few seconds to realize that it's the sound of M's laughter.

"Nah. Just something I know about. Remember...I'm a knower. It belonged to a sad old man who was fond of wearing ugly brown suits. He's long dead now and he doesn't need it anymore. It's all yours, Roman."

My fist is wrapped tightly around the cash. This will pay the utility bill and get the lights back on and then some.

"But nothing in this world is free. You best of all should understand that..."

The statement comes out of the hole and lingers there, sounding salacious and sinister. I'm starting to think maybe I should just put the money back where I found it and leave this place. Maybe nail the door shut forever too while I'm at it.

"What do you want for it?"

For a long time there is no answer.

I start to think that maybe M isn't there anymore.

"A friend."

Chapter 13

Roman

I staggered out of that root cellar into the openness of the world beyond, still reeling from everything I'd heard down there. It wasn't so much what I'd seen. There was almost nothing to see but a crack in the dirt. It was what came out of that chasm that stuck with me. I had absolutely no idea what it was that dwelled down there and I realize now that each time I even tried to ask that question M steered me away from it and changed the subject.

I upturned my face to the rain and let it wash across my dirt-smeared features. My right hand remained in my pocket, stroking the little bundle of bills that hid there. Something special was happening here. I didn't understand it. All I knew for sure was that things were looking up for Roman Merrick, and for now, that was enough.

All M claimed to want was a friend. He or she….or it…asked me to promise to visit frequently. I could do that. I'd tell no one about M. I wouldn't even mention it to my parents. Even if I tried to explain it to someone I knew it would be a fastrack to my very own padded room in the local asylum.

I decided then and there that I'd tell Helena that I was able to pawn that ring after all.

I'd focus on getting the lights back on and getting the family back on track.

We would endure.

Thanks to M…we would endure.

Chapter 14

Roman

It took less than a day to get the electric company to turn the lights back on with the money I found in that toolbox. I was even able to pay in advance for the month of December too. Dad's relief was a reward all by itself. Mom's thankful embrace made it even better.

We'd gained a period of respite.

The situation didn't seem so suffocating anymore, and for the first time in weeks I allowed myself to actually relax. I went into town and treated myself to a steak dinner at Mountainside Diner with a bit of the money that remained.

I sat there in my booth in the back, cutting into the medium rare meat and relishing the flavor as it assaulted my taste buds. Each bite was a little bloody. Each one more delicious than the last...

My thoughts inevitably circled back to M.

For awhile I entertained the idea that M might be a person living in some kind of undiscovered cavern beneath the house. Was that even possible? It seemed iffy. Especially because of those comments M had made about "humans and labels."

I mulled over the idea that maybe M was a ghost. I'm pretty open-minded when it comes to the paranormal, so the thought of some person buried beneath the house and haunting the spot where he or she was buried didn't seem terribly difficult for me to swallow.

Maybe that was it. Some restless spirit trapped down there in the dirt just looking for a little companionship. Might explain why M knew my name and other details about me without ever having to be told...

It was a theory, nothing more.

I didn't really have a clue what M was.

But I was starting to get a pretty clear idea of what M could do.

I'd visit him again tonight, per the arrangement

Chapter 15

Roman

I sat there on the cold ground in much the same position as last time. My overcoat was bundled across my shoulders and a woolen scarf was wrapped around my neck like a scratchy python. The flashlight was off, lying next to some broken cobblestones.

M didn't like artificial light.

Instead it was suggested that I light a few of the candles I'd dropped the last time I came here. I'd formed them into a little circle around the crack in the earth, little depressions of dirt forming natural holders for them.

Viscous yellow wax spread across the dirt in tendrils, unhealthy fingers reaching slowly across the soil, growing and growing. The candlelight cast strange shadows across the old wooden walls and painted my face, giving it a deeply orange glow. I was quiet, contemplative.

M didn't like the flashlight...but he seemed to enjoy the little flames.

I still couldn't see anything in the depths of that hole except for darkness descending and the occasional ragged root reaching out from the earthen walls. M hadn't spoken since mentioning the candles. If there was tension in this silence I didn't notice it. I felt...strangely soothed. Was that M's doing?

It seemed an unnatural feeling, such tranquility settling into my bones, almost like I was hypnotized by the hole and the little flames dancing around it.

M's voice caught me off guard. It was much like a lullaby floating up out of the dirt, coming to me from unknowable depths and telling me to just let myself drift. I let it happen. I let myself flirt with sleep but never truly fall into the heart of slumber. This was a pleasant, tingly doze...and it was a struggle to even formulate thoughts when in this kind of state.

"I trust your situation has improved a bit since the last time we spoke?"

I wet my lips to reply. My tongue felt dry and warm in my mouth, not much saliva to lubricate the words I was searching for.

"It has. Thank you for that..."

"It was the least I could do, Roman." M replied, silky and sympathetic.

Strangely the longer I spent in the presence of M the less cold I felt. My body felt comfortably numb to the frigid air that had to be circulating through the root cellar. It felt almost like M was weaving warmth in circular motions around me using nothing but the candle flames as a source.

"I mean that very literally. It was just a taste. Nothing but a preview of the treasures I can offer a man like you. This world is full of precious gifts, Roman...most of them buried and forgotten. You just have to know where to look..."

It was happening again. I could literally feel it. M steering me towards something, influencing me to follow the trail of bread crumbs he was leaving with each and every honey dipped word. I desperately wanted to know more about these "precious gifts"...but I also needed to understand what I was dealing with.

"What are you, M?" Are you a ghost?"

It took considerable effort just to get the question to leave my lips.

I waited. The minutes ticked by on my cheap wristwatch and M didn't respond. He hadn't gone away though. I could still sense him lingering somewhere down below. Apparently this was a topic M didn't want to talk about.

"Why are you down in that hole?"

A pause. It stretched on only a moment or two before the dirty sweet lullaby of M's voice returned to me.

"I'm trapped, Roman. A prisoner bound by walls of soil. The roots may as well be my steel bars, the dirt my three meals a day. I am shackled by earth and my only companions are sightless worms that aren't big on conversation."

40

There seemed such a tragic note to this admission. I was sad for M. I couldn't tell if it was genuine emotion or something M wanted me to feel...but regardless, I couldn't shake the melancholy. I couldn't imagine what it must be like to be trapped in such a cold, dark place.

"That's why I'm so pleased to have you now, Roman. Someone to talk with. Someone to share with. My new and special friend..."

A sigh emerged from the soil, wistful as it echoed up from that gaping darkness.

"Stick with me and you'll struggle no longer, Roman. The time for clawing and scraping for a meager meal is at an end. My table spills over...and you'll dine with me now."

The stale air of the root cellar seemed to crackle with possibilities. I leaned forward over the hole, listening intently.

"I'll feed you wealth and knowledge, child of flesh and sinew. I'll feed you pleasure and joy and all things men crave in this life. My whispers are all for you and only you...and they will lead you to great wonders."

A little shiver was traveling up my spine, warm and tingly. It was like being massaged from the inside, hideously pleasant.

"I want the struggle to be over, M. My family and I have struggled enough...but I have nothing to repay you with. Why do anything for me?" I asked.

"That's where you're wrong, child of flesh and sinew."

The candles began to sputter, the flames growing dim.

"If your mind remains open and your hands unfurl to do my work...then you have much to offer me."

I could feel the cold returning, M's voice fading. The sound of his words seemed to be coming from very far away now.

"Consider it a mutually beneficial relationship."

I felt that warm, slithery sensation departing my body.

"One last thing, Roman...the next time you visit...bring a shovel."

The little flames seemed to all wink out at once, the candles going dark and sending up little tendrils of smoke as they died. It seemed there was no more to be said for now.

M was gone.

Chapter 16

Roman

I slept badly that night. A hot, sticky sweat clung to my body as I tossed and turned in the bed. I seemed to always be on the edge of restful sleep before the memory of M's voice brought me back to reality. I felt panicked and excited and completely unsure of what comes next.

At some point I slipped off to fretful sleep. It gave me no comfort. I fell from a world of perspiration and uneasiness into a nest of sharpened dreams. My eyes opened to that other world I'd experienced once before in the dream that befell me in the cemetery. A place where the stars are too bright and the moon is too close.

I was in my own body and looking through my own eyes and I knew instantly that I was dreaming. I was in an ancient forest, the trees towering above me like monoliths. This was a time before man, an era before evolution had taken us from knuckle-dragging apes to the apex predators of planet Earth.

I was nude and using my hands to dig and claw at the dirt of the forest floor. I was smeared in the soil and blackened by it, my face feeling caked by the very ground itself. I could hear the chirps of strange insects all around me and even the distant roar of some animal that sounded horribly large.

My digging was frantic and I could do nothing to stop myself. My fingernails were broken and ragged, the blood from them dripping down into the dirt and giving it a crimson taint. I looked up and realized I was at least twenty feet deep into this hole.

I was tunneling deeper and deeper, the dirt flying out behind my shoulders, the hole becoming impossibly large. My hand seized a mole and squeezed until the very intestines of the rodent burst out from its nostrils. I had to keep digging. Nothing could stop me from getting down there.

It was my destiny lying in this dirt and I meant to claim it.

I was so far below now that no sunshine could penetrate the chasm I'd created. This was a dark hole made for dark things and light had no place within it. My bloody fingers pierced the soil to keep digging...but I touched something that did not yield.

Not rock, not some obstruction. It was warm, seeming to pulsate beneath my touch. It was flesh. The patchwork skin of something buried for millennia and freshly freed by my own hands.

My breath caught in my throat and in the next instant, my entire world exploded as something gargantuan burst out of the soil. I felt myself flying through darkness. When vision finally returned to me I was in a different place at a different time. I could feel it.

The only constant was that I was still buried, still embraced on all sides by gritty earth. But now...I was suspended above the inner confines of a rotten coffin. I seemed to float above the desiccated remains of a long dead corpse.

Even in the dream I could smell it and I struggled not to retch. I caught movements in the eyes and for a moment I mistakenly thought that the corpse was staring at me. I realized a few seconds later that clumps of tubifex worms had taken up residence in the empty hollows where the eyes had once been.

I wanted to wake up now. I wanted to wake up more than anything else in the whole wide world. I stared down at the corpse in the dirty brown suit and I tried to will myself out of that dank coffin, out of that grave, out of those stygian depths.

That's when the frail hand of the dead thing moved to the inner wall of the coffin. It moved slowly and strangely, the fingers plucking like something from a stop motion animation. It was scratching with fingernails that had grown even longer and sharper in the silence of the grave.

It took great effort from my frazzled mind to understand that the corpse was scratching a message for me. Words were taking shape in the rotten wood, ragged and full of dreadful weight.

The skeletal hand fell back down, the work of the fingernails done for the time being. I squinted through the blackness of the coffin to read what had been left for me there.

It was just a single line.

"He must remain below."

That's when the floating feeling left me. The soil around me began to crash down from all sides, pushing me deeper, burying me and cutting off all oxygen. My back was breaking from the weight of it and my nostrils felt full and I couldn't breathe because there was nothing but filth to fill my lungs.

I opened my mouth to scream and the sour soil poured in and choked me and choked me...and then finally awoke me.

I sat up in my own bed, the sheets plastered to my skin and soaked with sweat. I tore fresh air into my lungs and tried desperately to find even a semblance of composure.

I could still taste dirt on my tongue.

Chapter 17

Roman

The nightmare should have dissuaded me. Any sane, rational man would have laid boards across the little door of that root cellar and nailed it closed forever. A part of me felt like that's what I should be doing right now. Another part of me whispered that it wouldn't make any difference now.

Things had come this far. I'd crossed the Rubicon and I'd awakened M. Deep down inside I knew even if I turned away from his influence and tried to deny him he'd find a way to pull me back in. I didn't have the slightest idea how far M's reach could span but I'd seen a few examples of his power already. M was like some magical entity from a fairytale that could accomplish feats that men of flesh and bone can only fantasize about.

The corpse in the dirty brown suit was telling me to turn from the path...but I wasn't ready to do that just yet. And to be perfectly honest, I didn't want to abandon M and his promises. I was making a conscious decision to do what he wanted in an effort to ensure that this "mutually beneficial relationship" continued to thrive. This was my choice. It would either elevate me to levels I'd never even get close to without M's help...or it would bury me. I'd deal with those consequences later.

I was fueled by desperation. I was jobless and practically penniless with no hope on the horizon. I had a sick mother at home and a father who was breaking his back just to try and keep us crawling away from the shadow of financial ruin. I knew what waited in front of me if I shut out M's voice.

A future that involved begging for spare change and sleeping on the streets underneath thin cardboard blankets. I could expect a place in the world as one of the unseen and ignored, homeless and pathetic and dehumanized by poverty.

That was Option A. Listen to a dead man in a dirty brown suit, the ghost that lived only in my dreams...and let him lead me into obscurity.

And then there was Option B. Listen to M. Let the wealth of the world wash over me, let my desires be fulfilled and let my life mean something. It was the far more tempting option and in my mind, it was the only option.

I realized it was a bit greedy, a bit selfish...but I didn't care. I wanted something better for myself and my family. I was willing to go to whatever drastic lengths were necessary to ensure that our quality of life improved.

I wasn't content to just let myself fade into the gutters of hopelessness. Fuck that. This was my chance...and I intended to make the most of it.

These were the thoughts that circled through my head as I walked along the sidewalks of Rust Valley's main street. The town wasn't all that huge and most of the businesses were here in the town center. The sky was endlessly blue today and the clouds seemed especially white and fluffy, the air carrying that familiar bone-deep chill. My hands were shoved deep into the pockets of my overcoat and my head was lowered, not really paying much attention to my surroundings.

There was a shovel in the little shed at the house but the handle was badly splintered and the blade cracked. It wouldn't serve for whatever digging M had in mind for me. I needed a proper tool, something that would last.

I'd decided to buy a new one at the hardware store with what little money remained from the last paycheck I got before I lost my job. I didn't have much to spare, but I felt this investment would pay off in the long run.

I rounded a corner and headed towards the hardware store at the far end of the street when I noticed a familiar figure sitting on the bench along the sidewalk. Her long black hair tousled by the wind, her light gray eyes focused on the book that she held mere inches from her face. She bit her lip just slightly, giving me the idea that she'd gotten to a particularly good part in the story.

She wore all black, as per usual. A wooly black sweater and tattered fishnet beneath a dark plaid skirt. Her combat boots were scuffed and worn, the black polish on her fingernails chipped and picked at. Her glasses were big and the lenses thick, making those gray eyes seem infinitely larger and brimming with curiosity. She was so pale that her skin seemed almost translucent when the hard November sunshine fell down upon it.

Rose Crimshire was the only goth girl in a town that favored camouflage and four wheelers and all things country fried. She stuck out like a sore thumb, the perfect outcast. We weren't exactly close friends. She always struck me as a very private person, almost unknowable in her own way. We were cordial to one another though and we often talked a little when we saw each other. I guess I'd consider her an acquaintance. Those people that flit in and out of your life from time to time, you enjoy them when they're around but you don't really notice when they're not around.

We went to the same high school together a few years ago and I knew that Rose worked at the library a few streets over. She was often tortured in high school, the bullying so disgusting that it made my blood boil. Her pale arms were scratched and scarred all the time. Rose cut herself...and back in high school she earned the nickname Thorny Rose. Some of the crueler kids in school would taunt and catcall her in the hallways.

"Did you prick yourself today, Thorny Rose?"

"Gross, see her forearms? Trim those thorns!"

These kind of taunts would follow her wherever she went, her pretty little pixielike face concealed by a veil of black hair. One time I'd stepped in and tried to stop it. A fat bully named Lester had Rose backed up into a locker, running grubby hands through her hair and asking her to show him where the thorns got her. I was pretty quiet in high school, mostly kept to myself when not with my little circle of friends, but something came over me at that moment.

It was like a slow burning rage that scorched through my soul and I launched myself at the kid, throwing body shots left and right into his girth while yelling "Leave her alone!" He was stunned, the look of surprise passing across his fleshy face almost comical.

I ended up getting my ass beat in the end because Lester outweighed me by almost 150lbs, but I got a few good shots in. He had a bloody lip when he finally lumbered away and I savored that little victory.

Rose helped me up and showed me something that I'd never seen before. Her smile. It lit up her whole face like a brilliant crescent moon. The little nests of acne on her temples and the dark hollows beneath her eyes didn't matter. At that moment, smiling at me in that hallway...she was beyond beautiful.

That memory was fresh in my mind even though it happened awhile ago. Years had passed since then and high school was just a piece of the past now. Rose's head tilted up from her book as I walked closer, and that same little smile appeared across her face. Tiny white teeth and playful upturned lips.

I wasn't all that surprised to see that her smile had the same effect on me now as it did then.

The passage of time can change many things...but not the beauty of a familiar smile. It's just a little expression of happiness on someone's face that provokes the same feeling inside of you when you see it, but it means so much. There's something eternal about that kind of smile.

Chapter 18

Roman

"Hey, Ro..."

She never used my full name. There was something endearing about that, almost like Ro was something just between us. It was approaching late evening now and the sun was low in the sky, the glare of it catching in the thick lenses of her glasses.

"Good to see you, Rose. Little cold out here for reading, isn't it?"

Her smile transformed into a little smirk. There was light acne scarring along her cheeks and the dimples that formed there looked delightfully mischievous.

"I don't mind the cold so much. The library can get a little musty sometimes and the fresh air is nice. I can tolerate discomfort if the reward is worth it."

She was weird. I liked weird, though. My eyes wandered down to her sleeves for a moment, lighting upon the crisscrossed scars that ran up her wrist and forearms. She must have caught me looking because she self-consciously pulled the material of her sweater down a bit more. Rose had always hated her scars.

"What about you, Ro? Off to the cemetery to trim hedges and commune with the dead?"

I chuckled, shaking my head slowly.

"Not anymore. There's no more work there now that the season has ended. They let me go..."

She reached up to push a lock of black hair behind her ear, the wind immediately dislodging it and causing it to twirl again. She didn't bother a second time.

"That blows. The guy who runs the place is a dick anyways. I used to walk by his office on my way home sometimes and I'd catch a glimpse of him through the window rubbing himself through his khaki shorts and watching 1970s porn."

Rose mimed putting her finger down her throat and retching.

"Hey, don't knock it...that stuff is gold. Moustaches for days and really awkward close-ups. They were devoted to their craft!"

Rose clamps her book shut and places it down on the bench beside her, a little chortle of laughter flowing out past lips painted a dark crimson. I noticed she was reading Horns by Joe Hill. A good choice.

"Gross. So where are you going then, oh mysterious one?"

I nodded towards the hardware store down the street. I didn't want to say too much about what I was going to get there. I liked Rose, but I certainly couldn't confide in her about M. I felt that I could confide in absolutely no one when it came to M. It was critical that everything about that root cellar and what lived below needed to remain a secret.

"Just running some errands, gonna pick up some stuff for dad."

"Mmm. Nothing says father and son bonding time like hammering and sawing and all that good shit."

"For sure. If we end up building an ark together I'll save you a VIP spot on it."

That little smirk again, the adorable dimples on full display. I'd always joke with her about Bible-related stuff. Rose was a hardcore atheist and I wasn't religious one way or the other, so it seemed a funny topic to play around with. Almost everyone in this town was a Christian so we definitely fell into the minority.

"Such a sweetheart. I'll bring an armful of serpents with me and we'll make it a real party, kay?"

I had started to walk off while chuckling, offering Rose a little wave as I headed down the sidewalk. She returned the wave and picked her book back up into her lap. She called out to me as I was crossing the street...

"Hey, Ro! Text me sometime, yeah? It's been too long. We need to hang."

I flashed her a thumbs up while walking backwards towards the opposite sidewalk.

"Way too long! I'll do that."

I spun around and kept walking towards the hardware store. Truthfully I had no intention of texting Rose anytime soon. My mind was fixed on other things right now. Thoughts of dirt and shovels and ghosts and voices from the deep.

I didn't spend long in the hardware store. I chose one of the best shovels I could afford. The old-timer at the cash register assured me that it was a top of the line tool. Stainless steel and sturdy as can be, it would help me tear through just about any surface.

I had no doubt the shovel would be up to the task.

Now I just needed to figure out exactly what that task was...

Chapter 19

Roman

I waited for nightfall. I trudged through the dead leaves and the surviving vegetation surrounding the entrance to the root cellar. I nicked my neck across a large thorn bush, a tiny bead of blood appearing on my flesh. I swiped it away without even breaking stride. I made good use of the shovel, chopping and fighting my way through the overgrowth.

My boot came down into a little pool of hidden stagnant water and I felt my sock get soaked through. It was a squishy, uncomfortable sensation...but it didn't matter. All that mattered was the small door that I now stood in front of.

I pushed it inward and entered, the scent of M's lair filling my nostrils. The smell of sickly sweet soil gave me momentary pause. I took care in closing the door behind me before turning back around and letting my eyes settle on that crack in the earth. So easy to miss and overlook, just a few inches across on each side.

I didn't know what to expect...but what happened next certainly wasn't what I was banking on. I got the profound sense of something *rushing* upwards through the dirt below me, the speed of it frantic and excited. The weight beneath me shifted so much that a few little plumes of dust fell down from the root cellar's ceiling. The world beneath my boots seemed to actually be vibrating.

M's voice followed, sounding closer to the crack in the dirt than ever before. It was booming, ear-splitting...nothing like that silky purr I'd become accustomed to. I staggered backwards into the wall at the sound of it.

"YOU'RE BLEEDING, ROMAN. TORN FLESH..."

I almost got the sense of M breathing somewhere below, his lungs (if he even had lungs) like giant air balloons expanding at a quickened pace.

"...how do you know that?"

"I can smell it, Roman. It's been a long time since I've caught the blood scent."

M's voice sounded calmer when he replied, almost like it was taking him a great deal of effort to control himself.

"Come closer, Roman."

I didn't want to come closer. The familiar fear was roiling in my guts. I'd become a bit desensitized to M because of all of the conversations we'd had, but now that fear of the unknown came flooding back in, threatening to drown me.

I had no fucking idea what I was dealing with here. I didn't know what this thing was or what it wanted. If I was smart, I'd run now...

"Trust is important in any relationship, child of flesh and sinew. Trust in me."

I swallowed dryly, my grip on the shovel handle tightening.

"Closer."

I took a shaky step forward, and then another.

"I brought the shovel, just like you wanted..." My voice felt weak exiting my throat, barely above a hoarse whisper.

"That's good. We'll get to that. Closer, Roman."

I was standing right above the hole now, and there seemed to be an eerie wind swirling around within it. It blew back my hair and then moments later it turned inward, a few specks of dirt falling down into the chasm. I could still see nothing down there, only blackness.

"Kneel down."

That trance seemed to be settling over me again like hands massaging me from the inside. It was comforting...like a subliminal message repeating over and over again in my head, telling me "everything is okay."

I knelt down before the hole, my hands so tight on the shovel handle that my knuckles had gone white. That wind came again. It was so strong that it seemed to dry out every pore on my face. It stank too. It stank of death and decay and ancient, unexplored abysses.

"What is this, M?"

"Shh. Trust, Roman."

I closed my mouth, afraid to protest anymore. I was at M's mercy now.

"Touch the wound. Get the blood onto your hand. Pretend like you're a little kid again and it's time for finger-painting..."

This statement sent a deeper chill into my body, but I was already complying, my hand reaching up to rub against the smeared blood on the side of my neck.

It was still very wet and felt warm to the touch. The little cut had produced more plasma than I'd expected.

"Now...flick the droplets down to me, Roman. Quickly."

That wind was overpowering now, sucking in and blowing outward. I made a terrible realization at that moment. It wasn't wind. It was M breathing from deep within the pit. He'd climbed up as close to the crack as he could get...and he was relishing the blood scent.

I wanted to get it over with. If I was going to be pulled down there and something unmentionable was about to happen to me, I didn't want to drag it out and suffer in suspense.

I flicked my hand in a downward motion, a few little blood rubies flying from my fingertips and entering into the chasm. Nothing happened for a moment. The silence was too much to bear. Then the silence was broken by a long, drawn out satisfied sigh...seeming to stretch on and on.

The sound of M's elation.

"Thank you for that. Just a little taste...but it brings back memories."

I sensed M descending deeper and deeper, his presence still lingering near the opening in the dirt but not nearly as close as before. Some of the tension went out of my muscles. I felt if M had wanted to kill me at that moment then I'd already be mince meat.

"Now...let's put that shovel to use, shall we? Start digging, my fine young friend. Put your back into it and do your best work. You'll be paid handsomely...I don't believe in the concept of minimum wage!"

I stood back up, leaning heavily on the shovel to keep my balance. I still felt a bit shaky but my composure was returning, albeit slowly.

"Dig where?"

"The hole, Roman..."

A pause, little motes of dust floating through the air of the root cellar and shining in what little moonlight managed to enter through the cracks in the walls.

"I need you to widen the hole."

A part of me had hoped that M wanted me to bring the shovel so that he could tell me where I needed to dig for buried treasure. There was another part of me, though...that knew deep down this is what M would want. M said he was trapped down there, a prisoner in the dirt. He wanted my help to gain his freedom...

I'd come this far. I'd crossed the Rubicon. No going back now...

I planted the blade of the shovel next to the crack and drove it down with my boot as hard as I possibly could.

Chapter 20

Roman

I worked fast, my breathing paced and deliberate. A cold sweat broke out across my skin and I had to stop several times to swipe my brow. The soil of the root cellar was hardened, challenging to dig through...but it softened as I got through the first few layers of topsoil. There was no commentary from M as I dug. He was deathly silent; the only sound in the root cellar the grunts of my exertion and the shovel blade slicing into the grit of the earth.

I'd widened the hole significantly; the crack now stripped enough for a small child to be able to crawl down into it. The smell from the pit below was stronger now. I was able to get a better idea of just how far down it went too. It was jagged and seemingly bottomless down there, something like an endless tunnel stretching down into pitch darkness.

I'd rolled my shirt up to the forearms and the soil was grimed across my arms, my fingernails crusted over with the dirt of the cellar. I was just about to impale the earth with the shovel once again when M's voice stopped me.

"That's enough for now."

I wiped my hands across my jeans, leaving dark smudges across the denim.

"Well done, Roman. Exceptional progress..."

I swung the shovel up over my shoulder and cocked my head to the side.

"What happens now?" I inquired.

"Now you get compensated. See that chunk of cobblestone? It's close to the hole."

I surveyed the area, noticing a chunk that seemed to be in a different position than the last time I was here. It was close to the hole I'd made and near one corner of the cellar.

"The one near the corner?"

"Bingo. Take a peek underneath."

I tossed the shovel to the side and moved over to the cobblestone, proceeding to lean down. I reached down towards the fragment of stone and flipped it to the side. It wasn't all that heavy.

I didn't realize what I was seeing at first. I was looking at a clump of dirt and mineral rock, glittery yellow staring up at me from the center of it. I picked it up; awestruck...and realized I was holding a piece of rock in my hand that was shot through with a vein of gold. My jaw dropped open as I marveled at the little nuggets encircled by pieces of quartz.

"Is this...is this gold?" I asked, still disbelieving what I was seeing.

M's laughter greeted me, melodic and pleasing to the ears.

"It is, Roman. Remember what I said, the ground is full of precious gifts just waiting to be unearthed. Consider this a bit of motivation to keep up the good work you've started here."

I was turning over the chunk of minerals in my hand, trying to mentally appraise just how much this material could be worth. I couldn't even imagine.

"Shift's over, buddy. Take the spoils of your labor and go enjoy yourself for a few days, yeah?"

M was leaving again, that slithery shift felt through subtle vibrations beneath my feet. His voice drifted up as a hollow whisper, circling through my mind as I lovingly held the gold closer to my eyes.

"Get some rest after, though. We're just getting started..."

The root cellar went quiet. The hole I'd widened seemed to gape like a wordless mouth. I shoved the payment into my pocket and let my hand follow it in, continuing to explore and touch the surface of it.

This would change everything. I knew that almost immediately. The rules of the game had changed. The weight of the precious thing in my pocket served only to reinforce that.

M promised great wealth...limitless generosity.

He was starting to deliver.

57

Chapter 21

Roman

It didn't take long to get the chunk of gold-rich ore appraised. It was even easier getting it sold. The comforting weight of it in my pocket was gone, replaced by seventeen thousand dollars. I had to keep repeating that number over and over again in my mind to actually convince myself that this was happening. Seventeen thousand dollars. Cold, hard, wonderful cash. It was crisp and it smelled so perfectly new. That first night I couldn't help myself, I gave in to the old clichés and I spread out a bouquet of currency across my bed and then flung myself backwards into it. I rolled around in it. I relished the feel of it against my skin. I brought handfuls of it up to my nostrils and inhaled so deeply, the intoxicating scent hitting me harder than the hardest of street drugs.

I'd discovered a new addiction. It was green and precious and covered in the faces of dead presidents. It was everything in this world...and it was something I never had an abundance of up until this very moment. They say money is the doorway to corruption, but the thing they don't tell you is that you don't even notice when you've crossed through the threshold of that doorway.

You're too euphoric to even think about it, wallet fat and mind racing with possibilities.

I'd spared no expense on the Thanksgiving spread that was now laid out on the kitchen table before us. Succulent turkey, glazed ham, mountains of stuffing and bountiful plates heaped high with green beans and mashed potatoes. This was the kind of feast that my family deserved, and it felt so empowering to be able to provide it for them. My parents had noticed that something drastic had changed in my financial situation but they couldn't figure out exactly what it was. I was concerned that they'd think I was getting this money from some criminal venture, like theft or drug dealing...so I devised another little white lie to protect the incomprehensible truth.

My father cut deeply into the ham, bringing mouthful after mouthful up to his bearded mouth. My mother was busying herself buttering up a crisp biscuit, the color back in her cheeks this evening. I took a moment just to appreciate my family. It was good to see them happy and fulfilled.

I planned to do everything within my power to ensure that they stayed that way.

"So you've probably been wondering how I've been able to afford all this..."

I let the statement linger, Braham pausing to meet my eyes. Helena finished a piece of her biscuit and then wiped her mouth with a napkin before favoring me with her attention as well. Dad was the first to reply.

"We love you, son. I can't remember the last time this table was so plentiful on Thanksgiving...and your mother and I really appreciate that..."

He left off, seeming to choose his words carefully.

"But understand that you don't need to get into something dangerous to put food on the table for us. You know we can make due when times get hard. We have before. It's not worth losing you...and it ain't worth losing yourself in whatever put this money in your pocket."

I nodded, my head momentarily lowering. I found it hard to meet my father's eyes when he made this admission. I wished I could tell them the truth to ease the worry growing in their hearts, but I could see no sane way of explaining what was actually happening with me.

Helena chimed in to break the silence, my eyes tilting upwards once again.

"Listen to your old dad, Roman. We taught you to earn things the right way, son. Never think that you have to resort to something that'll get you into trouble just to get by. That's a dark road to go down...and the trip ain't even halfway worth it."

She leaned forward to place her hand overtop mine. I turned it over and squeezed it. Tears threatened to fall down my mom's cheeks at any moment, but she held them back valiantly.

"It's nothing like that, guys. I didn't get this money by going against the law. I waited for a special occasion to tell you...but I found a job. It's part time work with a private mining company, but it has some perks. If the workers find any nuggets during the shift then you get to keep what you find as long as you give the proper percentage back to the company. That's where this money came from..."

I smiled. It felt reassuring and strong on my face. I hoped sincerely that it masked the lie I was telling.

"I've got a real nose for this kind of work. My foreman says I can practically sniff out the ore. It pays off for everybody. It's kind of a situation where they scratch my back if I scratch theirs."

My father's expression had changed. The doubt in his eyes had transformed into newfound hope. My mother squeezed my hand tighter, a gesture of pride in her son and his accomplishments.

"Roman...that's the best damn news we've had all year, son. It's about time our luck took a turn!"

Dad clapped me on the back; the hand calloused by year after year of toiling hard to keep this family afloat. Mom was already rising from her chair to wrap her arms around me in a tight hug. My arms automatically reached out to return her embrace. She whispered into my ear, her voice choked with emotion.

"Thank the lord, my prayers are answered. I knew my boy was meant for big things in life. So proud of you, Roman..."

I sat there, accepting the love and pride from my family. It took every amount of willpower to remain calm and collected on the surface. Deep down inside I was a little sickened with myself for feeding my parents lies right along with Thanksgiving supper. The feeling was a bitter shame in my belly...but it didn't last long. I knew that with all these little white lies cast aside, my intentions were good. We were thriving. We were happy. The where and the why of everything didn't matter so much right there and then.

And there was a smidgen of truth to what I said. It was a situation where if I scratch a back then my back is scratched in return. The only detail I neglected to tell them was that it was M's back that I was scratching...and his unseen claws were scratching mine.

This was the time of year set aside for counting your blessings and being thankful for all the positive things in your life. I was thankful this year.

I was thankful for M.

I even flirted with the idea of taking a plateful of turkey out to M and dropping it down into his hole after supper. Best not, though. Seemed kinda like throwing scraps to a dog. M might be offended...

I raised my fork and knife and smiled at my folks, my attention returning to the plate full of hot, delicious food sitting in front of me. I smiled wide, unmindful of the little pieces of turkey gristle stuck in my teeth.

"Let's eat."

Chapter 22

Roman

The dishes were washed and the table cleared, the folks sitting down in front of the television and relaxing a bit. I was finishing up placing some leftovers into the fridge when I got the idea to give those stray kittens outside a few pieces of turkey too. They were mostly feral except for one little guy who was tame compared to the others. He'd let himself be petted and mom had taken a shine to him, even got a cute little black collar for him with a bell on it.

Whenever I'd open the side door for something I'd hear that bell jingling as he ran over to greet me. That's how he earned the name Mr. Jingle.

I fixed him a little Thanksgiving dinner to share with his brothers and sisters, putting a few of the tastier morsels into a Rubbermaid container. I shrugged one of my heavier coats on and headed out through the side door, the little porch light casting a weak bit of illumination over the gathered shadows. It was only a little after 5pm but darkness came early this time of year in Rust Valley. The daylight never lasted long in the winter months so those precious hours had to be savored.

The door slammed shut behind me without any effort on my part; the wind took care of it for me. I headed in the direction of that tattered old upside down couch near the side of the house. The litter of kittens usually took shelter under there. Usually they'd catch the scent of food and come running immediately...but strangely enough the area around the couch was silent.

I knelt down and called out, even proceeded to toss a few chunks of turkey meat on the ground near the couch. No kittens greeted me. There were no jingling bells and no expectant meows. The only sound was the wind, hollow and wispy.

I pushed back up to my feet and started to walk around, wondering if the kittens had relocated to some new little lair near the house. I tromped through the bushes and found myself nearing the entrance to the root cellar. The ground here was always mucky and wet...and I immediately noticed little paw prints in the mud leading towards the root cellar's door.

It was open just a crack...enough for a tiny furry body to enter through the threshold. There was a nasty feeling in the pit of my stomach when I saw those paw prints. It was like anxious hands clenching and unclenching in the fibers of my gut. I didn't know if I wanted to open that door just now. I didn't know if I'd like what I found...

Nevertheless I found myself passing through the door and into M's territory. It was very dark in here now and almost no moonlight passed through the cracks in the walls. I had to squint and stumble before my sight finally adjusted a bit to the blackness. I could usually feel it when M was aware of my presence. It was a bizarre, indescribable sensation that would settle into my bones.

I wasn't experiencing that sensation now. I got the distinct vibe that M might be sleeping somewhere below, just as he was when I first discovered him.

I neared the crack in the earth, the one I'd widened considerably with nothing but a single shovel and my own manpower. The tiniest glimmers of moonlight managed to pierce through the rotten wood of the walls.

It was weak, paltry light...but it was enough.

It showed me things that I didn't want to see.

It showed me little tufts of cat hair close to the crack in the dirt.

It shined on Mr. Jingle's collar snagged on a piece of root on the side of the descending pit.

And further down, as far as my vision could reach...it showed me the worst thing of all. A tiny little rope of intestine plastered across the earthen wall and marinating in a smear of fresh cat blood.

A trembling hand rose to cover my mouth and I was already starting to stagger back up to my feet. I started backing up slowly to the door, tiptoeing to keep M ignorant of my presence. I didn't want to awaken him. Not now...not after seeing this.

All I wanted right at this moment was to get the hell out of this root cellar and empty the contents of my stomach into the bushes outside.

I stumbled and staggered and clawed the door open.

I fell to my hands and knees in the mud, my gorge rising, my throat working. I started to retch, the slimy bile beginning to gurgle forth from deep within. A stream of turkey and stuffing flavored vomit belched forth out of my lips and splattered across the undergrowth surrounding M's front door.

I stared down at the pool of my own puke for a few seconds, disgusted by the sight of everything I'd eaten today. Simply the concept of eating disgusted me right now. It was all too much to bear. It only served to remind me...

M had celebrated Thanksgiving with a feast of his own.

Chapter 23

Roman

I needed time to think. I did my best thinking while driving, and that's why I now found myself cruising along deserted back roads with the headlights cutting through the darkness ahead of me. One hand loosely gripped the steering wheel; the other was busy massaging my temple. My stomach still felt weak and knotted. I was having a hard time formulating coherent thoughts, my mind inevitably circling back to that image of Mr. Jingle's blood-stained collar.

I'd aligned myself with something that I did not understand. I was working with a thing that devoured kittens. I let that sink in for a moment. It made me feel like an extremely shitty human being. I'd been afraid of M, I'd been curious about M...but this was the first time I'd actually considered M evil.

Anything that would mutilate something so innocent had to be evil. The torn entrails, the ripped out fur...that trusting little cat shredded into bite-size pieces.

The moment M asked me to flick some of my blood down to him should have tipped me off. I should have realized then that whatever this thing was, it had an appetite. It apparently had a stomach to digest with and a body to contain that stomach. I'd ruled out that M was any kind of ghost now...just didn't seem to make sense.

I was no closer to figuring out what M was or what M's motives were. Every question just leads me to more questions. All I knew for sure was that M wanted out of that dirt. He'd been trapped in that underground prison for who knows how long and he needed my help to crawl his way up to the surface.

Was I willing to continue helping him? Did I even have the vaguest concept of what I might be unleashing upon the world?

I didn't. I needed answers. I needed to dig down to the truth before I dug down any deeper into that root cellar soil.

Right now all I had on my hands was the blood of a little animal, but if I kept on this current course, I might find my hands soaked and stained forever.

I like to think I'm a good man. I like to think that my intentions are good. All I want is a better life for me and mine. But I'm not willing to sacrifice lives, big or small, to obtain that better life. Just like my mom said...it's not worth losing yourself down that dark road. If you lose your way on that kind of road there's a damn good chance you may never find your way back again.

I needed to confront M.

I had to gather my courage and force every scrap of willpower I had to spare into my heart, and I had to march into that root cellar and take a stand.

It might lead to the end of our "mutually beneficial relationship" but there was something more important to me than all the gold and precious gifts M could unearth.

Something I could not let be shattered and forever ruined by my own poor choices. I had to keep it intact by any means necessary...

I had to keep my soul intact.

Chapter 24

Roman

I waited until after midnight before I drove back home. I waited until dad had gone off to work the night shift. I waited until mom was fast asleep, her medication usually causing her to sleep like the dead. I drove back fast down the dirt lane, dust pluming out behind the wheels. Poe's "Haunted" blasted out of the radio.

My jaw was clenched, my hands gripping tightly to the wheel. I wasn't afraid of what I had to do. I was angry. There was lead in my belly and fire in my eyes and I wanted nothing more than to stomp my way into that root cellar and scream down into M's hole until my lungs couldn't pull anymore air into them. Maybe it was silly to be so pissed off about the death of a little stray kitten. Maybe this whole situation was driving me crazy. I was angry at myself most of all for trusting in something that was perhaps beyond the scope of my understanding.

I was blinded by a rage that seemed to just swell up in me out of absolutely nowhere. I tore the wheel to the side and slammed the car into park, not even bothering to close the door or shut off the headlights. I stormed out of the Buick and marched across the yard. My boots crunched across wet grass, deep indentations left in the ground with each step that I took.

I was vaguely aware that my fists were clenched at my sides as I walked. The fingernails were biting into my flesh and I didn't care. I liked the pain at that moment. Something was happening here. I felt...a pull. I tried to clear my head and think about this rationally, but my mind seemed full of blistering red snakes that kept coiling around each other over and over again. I couldn't think. I couldn't strategize.

I reached the door and I tore it open, the hinges creaking in protest. I sauntered in and opened my mouth to roar out M's name...but I stopped with my lips just beginning to open.

All the candles had been replaced around the hole in the soil, a rudimentary circle surrounding it and casting long shadows across the walls. That sour stench wafted up from the pit, making my nostrils wrinkle. I was grinding my teeth like an animal. I never grinded my teeth. What the hell was wrong with me?

M's voice greeted me immediately, strong and expectant.

"Right on time."

He was waiting. He knew I'd be coming. This visit seemed almost...preplanned.

"Rage. It's the purest of human emotions. It's a cloud where all clarity is lost, but so much can be accomplished while in the grip of that cloud. Do you feel it, Roman? Are you swimming through the red...letting it overtake you?"

My nostrils flared. I was feeling it alright.

"What are you, M? No more games..." I asked, my voice a low growl in the back of my throat.

Laughter. The melody of M's merriment traveled through the cellar and echoed from the cavernous confines below.

"Why the cat? You wanted me to find that, didn't you?" I pressed, unwilling to be rebuked so quickly.

"Surely you don't mourn for that little creature, do you? A heart the size of a pebble and a life force that accounts to nothing. Not even a snack for me, Roman. Barely a crumb..."

The candle flames flicker, my shadow stretching out across the walls and seeming to pulsate right along with my heavy breathing.

"Consider it a reminder, child of flesh and sinew. Our deal will lead to bloodshed. There must be sacrifices along the way. My generosity has a price. Everything in this world and below this world has a price. Sometimes it will be nothing more than a crumb, as I've displayed for you..."

My anger was fading, replaced by a feeling of numbness.

"Other times it will be more. I am very old and very hungry; Roman...starved for centuries and forced to wallow with worms. I will walk your world again. This is a serious matter for a serious servant and there is no room for disobedience along the way."

That word hit me hard. M had called me his servant. The entire tone of this speech was taking a very sinister turn...

"You will dig and sometimes I will ask you to do more. Are you ready for the more, Roman? That is the point of all of this...the little kitty a small example of the more. You must break through the walls of your comfort zone for me...and the rewards you receive for that will be limitless."

"What do you mean by more?" The question felt dangerous the moment it escaped my lips.

I stared down into the gaping pit, the chasm seeming almost to mock me with silence and everlasting darkness.

"Tomorrow after sunset, you dig. The hole needs to be wider for what I need. For what I crave. My belly grumbles from the deep, child of flesh and sinew. I crave. First you dig...then we will arrive at the more."

I scrubbed a hand across my mouth, my lips feeling dry. I felt hollowed out by this conversation, left weak and submissive. I'd entered here a furious beast and I'd been reduced to a weak, helpless little thing. Much like a kitten...

"Do my work, Roman. The hands of mankind are made to do my work..."

M's voice didn't sound so silky now. It sounded like it was coming from horrible grinding machinery, like endless rows of teeth chattering and snapping against each other.

"But remember that you are not the first to weave my work. And if you cross me..."

There were scratching sounds from the deep. The earth vibrated as something sharp and ungodly sank into the walls of dirt far beneath my feet.

"You will not be the last."

There was nothing more after this. Those threatening words sank in and I felt as though all the strength was about to go out of my legs. Dominance had been established on this night. I had been reminded of my place in M's machinations.

I turned to leave, defeated. My shoulders slumped as I exited the cellar.

The last sound I heard as I left was the tinkling of Mr. Jingle's bell somewhere in the bowels of the earth.

Chapter 25

Roman

I spent the following day in a haze. My folks attempted to communicate with me but soon they gave up after I just kept feeding them one word answers. I spent most of the morning and afternoon in bed, staring at the TV but not really paying attention to any of the monotonous images flashing across it.

I was demoralized. Nothing mattered. I was acutely aware of the passage of time. The hours and the minutes ticked away and each tick of the clock was like a steel fork stabbing down into my nerves. I was waiting for sundown.

I wanted nothing more than to crawl beneath the blankets on my bed and sleep for a month. Maybe then this nightmare I'd become embroiled in would end and I'd wake up refreshed and free of M's influence.

A lovely fantasy, but that's all it was...just a fantasy.

Evening had transformed into twilight. The purgatory of my waiting had ended.

I showered quickly, the hot water blasting across my face and running down the musculature of my chest. I stayed beneath the water for far too long in an attempt to put off the inevitable. By the time I dried off and stared at myself in the mirror my skin was beet red, my eyes staring out from dark hollows.

No more stalling.

It was tIme for my night work to begin.

Chapter 26

Roman

I was digging. The cords stood out on my neck and the sweat glistened along my torso. I'd stripped off my coat and the t-shirt beneath, my bare skin shiny with the perspiration of my labor. I should have been freezing down here, but I wasn't. I felt like I was in a boiler room. The heat seemed to bake up from beneath and hit me in waves.

M had said only one word when I arrived here. No greeting, no conversation. Only a command from under the soil...driven into my skull like a railroad spike being pounded in with a sledgehammer. It repeated itself periodically in the center of my brain, becoming much like a chant.

"Dig."

And so I was digging. M was humming from the depths of the earth, the melody seeming strangely sweet, but underlying that sweetness was a monotonous buzzing sound like legions of flies hatching and taking flight.

My muscles ached and my head was pounding but still I fought to gain more ground. The dirt was my enemy and I was hacking at it with the blade of the shovel, sending mounds of it flying out over my shoulder into one corner of the root cellar. Occasionally the shovel blade would sever through the segmented length of an earthworm. I'd watch it writhe for a moment, vivisected and ruined, before continuing to dig. M would giggle each time I sliced through a worm.

His giggle was like a choir of children all laughing together from a mass unmarked grave. It sent cold chills up my spine, but still the shovel fell. I never stopped to rest. Each time I felt the urge to take a little break that inner voice would whisper "dig" and I'd find myself complying without even questioning it.

The hole was widening quickly. I was up to my waist in depth and I had to keep both feet firmly planted on either side of that yawning abyss. The earthen walls down there had a strange circular appearance, rounded off at the sides. I assumed they'd gained that shape whenever M burrowed his way closer to the opening.

M's purr stopped me just as I was about to sink the shovel into another section of soil. It sounded perfectly relaxed and satisfied.

"You've been busy," said the thing from below.

I wiped my forehead, little pieces of grit falling down to catch in my eyelashes.

"Climb out and take a look. Take pride in your labor."

I hauled myself out of the hole and looked down into it, my feet at the edge of the opening. The hole resembled the kind of grave I used to dig when I worked at the cemetery, rectangular and descending down several feet. It had progressed so far from that little crack in the dirt...

"I see I've chosen the right man for the job..."

I stepped back from the grave-shaped pit I'd made and sank the shovel down into the dirt, allowing it to remain there.

"What happens now?" I asked.

"Now I think you should remove that rock from your shoe. I'd imagine it's a bit uncomfortable."

I wasn't aware of any rock in my shoe up until M mentioned it. I felt it now, though. It was jagged and biting up against my heel. I leaned down and dug down into my boot, proceeding to pull out the dirt-encrusted piece of rock.

It looked wrong, though. At first I thought it had pierced my heel and drawn blood. That might account for the reddish color. There was no lasting pain in my foot though, no plasma on the rock either. The crimson hue was coming from behind the crust of dirt. I begin picking off the flakes of earth and uncovering more of the rock's surface.

I brought it closer to my eyes, momentarily stunned.

It was a ruby the size of a baby's fist.

"Never know what kinda prize you're gonna get when you reach down into my cereal box, do you, kiddo?"

M's laughter serenaded me. I barely heard it; still busy marveling at the precious stone I was holding in my hand.

"Speaking of cereal...and food in general, that brings me to the next step, Roman. Are you ready for the next step?"

I nodded, my fist closing around the ruby.

"Meat is the next step, child of flesh and sinew. A substantial meal to quell an everlasting appetite. A crumb won't do this time. I need a large beast of the earth, meat that still lives and breathes when it is brought to my doorstep."

My eyes narrowed. I didn't like where this was going...

"I like my steak rare, Roman. So rare that I can see the terror in the eyes before I eat the eyes. Flesh that is raw, meat that moves in my mouth."

"What...kind of meat are you talking about?" I asked, my stomach tying itself up in knots all over again. I got the very strong feeling that M wasn't talking about an innocent trip down to the grocery store or the butcher's shop.

"Consider yourself my delivery boy, child of flesh and sinew. You'll bring my supper to me and I'll tip you like you've never been tipped before. You've widened the hole *just enough* for me to fit a little piece of myself out of it, Roman. You bring me what I need..."

What the hell did M mean by that? I'd widened the hole enough for him to squeeze a bit of himself through?

"I'll come up for a little fresh air...and I will feed. Very simple and easy. I need the energy. All these centuries of imprisonment have sapped me of my strength and I need protein to regain it. Bring me a walking steak...that'll be a damn good start."

"Are you talking about a cow?"

"Mhm. A living, breathing cow. The fatter the better. Just lead it to the slaughter, Roman. Humans devour these bovines every single day. You don't get sentimental about gobbling down a burger, do you?"

This wasn't exactly the same as the kitten. It wasn't a request that scraped too deeply against my moral compass, but that didn't make it any less bizarre.

"How the hell am I supposed to get a living cow down here? Where am I supposed to get a cow in the first place?"

"I don't know, farmer fuckin' Brown...FIND ONE. That's your task. Search the fields and bring it to the killing field. All you have to do is get it close to the hole."

I could almost hear the hunger in M's voice.

"I'll take care of the rest."

The doubt was creeping in, this entire scenario just seeming like too much for me.

"I don't know..."

"Do this, Roman...and you will die an old, rich man in a mansion on the hill with a healthy, happy family. Your children's children will prosper and your bloodline will never want for anything. But if you turn from the path...if you break our covenant..."

A sound like an impossibly large tongue scraping against tombstone teeth echoed up from the grave-hole.

"It will get ugly."

Images begin flashing through my head. My sick mother resting in her familiar chair. My father cleaning toilets in some nasty restroom. And finally an image of myself convulsing in the gutter, my body emaciated and my eyes rolled up to the whites as sewer rats danced across my pallid flesh.

I wasn't sure if these images came from my own imagination or if M planted them there, but regardless they haunted me.

It was only a cow. People ate cows all the time. They were livestock. It was just the nature of the world. It was all part of the food chain...

I wasn't willing to sacrifice everything that I loved in life for a fucking cow.

"I'll do it."

Chapter 27

Roman

I spent the next day driving around Rust Valley and looking for nearby fields that might harbor cattle. I was wearing a black hoodie with the hood pulled down low and thick aviator shades. I'd tried to conceal my identity as much as possible, but looking at myself in the rear view mirror I thought I was the spitting image of a stalker. I wasn't preying on beautiful women though or creeping outside of some celebrity's house.

I was stalking cows.

The very idea of this seemed both ridiculous and surreal all at the same time. I had no plan when it came to transporting the cow back to the root cellar. It wasn't like I could just shove the beast into the trunk and cruise off while whistling innocently...

I had more than enough cash on me to buy a cow (or a whole herd for that matter) but I didn't want to risk that. The farmer would likely remember me and I didn't want to leave any kind of paper trail. The last thing I needed was a rumor circulating in town that I was some kind of cow killer or cow fucker or god knows what...if mountain folk are good at anything, it's telling outlandish tales like that to stave off boredom.

This had to go down quietly. Today was just about scoping out the lay of the land and getting an idea of where I might be able to score a bovine. I had no intention of trying to pull it off during daylight hours. This would have to happen after sunset, just like most strange things do.

Just more night work to be done in the name of M's unknowable desires. I was starting to feel like some sort of nocturnal ghoul that gets down to nasty business when everyone else is fast asleep at home.

Most of the farms I saw were too far away from the root cellar. Some were closer but they were surrounded by other houses and it was likely I'd be spotted messing around in a field at night. I was starting to give up hope...

I was heading back down my lane and feeling defeated when I spotted the sprawling dirt road behind the "KEEP OUT" sign. I'd passed the entrance to this ragged little road before but I'd never really given it a second look. I had no idea what was down there. Figured it couldn't hurt to find out...

I ignored the sign's warning and drove down the road a bit. It was very dark, overhung with massive oak trees, the dead leaves crunching beneath the tires of my old Buick. I rounded a corner into a more open space and my eyes widened behind my sunglasses.

I'd hit the jackpot.

I found myself gazing out at a muddy brown field with yellowing grass and hills that sloped far over the horizon. There was a large farm house in the distance and I could just make out a barn and feed silo at the very extent of my vision, but all of that was far away from the field itself. The occupants of this field were all huddled in a tight circle near a large watering trough.

Big, beautiful cows...chewing cud and dropping steaming manure from behind swishing tails. There were plenty to choose from, little calves too, but what gave me pause was the big black bull that lingered at the edge of the circle. He might prove to be a complication. I'd have to find a way to deal with him if I wanted to be successful in bringing M what he asked for...

I stared at the grazing animals for a moment, wondering if they knew on some instinctual level that a predator was watching. They showed no sign of it if they did. They appeared calm and not even a little skittish, likely grown accustomed to humans being close by over the years. That would come in handy for me.

This was the place. This would be my hunting ground. When the moon rose higher and the blackness reigned, I would choose my sacrifice. I'd drive the car back home and walk back later when the time was right.

M would have his meat.

And when it's done, I'll have my family...and hopefully my sanity.

Chapter 28

Roman

Darkness fell. The moon shined bright tonight and it gave me all the light I'd need. I peered out from the edge of a wooded area that gave me a perfect vantage of the field. I was bundled from head to toe in black, my overcoat drawn tight and my hood pulled down low. I wore thick leather gloves and had a scarf wrapped around the lower half of my face. Even covered in so many layers the chill ran deep through my bones. I'd chosen a cold night for this task.

I was watching the cattle, hoping for that perfect straggler from the herd. I felt like a wolf hunkered down in the wilderness and looking for the easiest target. My eyes searched for limping legs, old and sick bovines...anything that wouldn't put up much of a fight when it was time to take it. I had a thick length of rope in my right hand for leading the cow back to the root cellar. I had no doubt in my mind I'd be leading it to the slaughter...

The herd was easy to see in the moonlight, clouds of cold breath expelled from many sets of wet nostrils. The beasts didn't move much; mainly they huddled together and shuffled their hooves occasionally. They were conserving body heat. I was well hidden and I didn't think they were aware of my presence, but even if they were they didn't seem to care that I was there.

There was one brown cow that seemed to stand apart from the others. She was clearly old, her body sagging with fat and her udders seeming to droop almost all the way down to the ground. She was busying herself by joylessly munching on what little yellow grass she could find on the outskirts of the herd. Her eyes seemed rheumy and clouded over with cataracts, giving me the idea that she was almost blind. There didn't seem to be much fight in this old girl...

Victim acquired, I tightened my grip on the length of rope in my hand. I approached as stealthily as possible, my footsteps light and my movements painstakingly quiet. There was some mild grunting from the herd as a few of them sighted me, but it didn't set off any kind of panic. They seemed completely indifferent to the sight of me approaching. I hadn't spotted the bull yet during this visit. I was starting to think I'd be able to pull this off without ever having to even interact with him...

I was in arm's length of the old brown cow now. Her head rose and she lowed at me, a dumb and oblivious sound. She then lowered her mouth back to the ground and began chewing at the grass again. I began to slowly circle the rope around her neck, making sure to knot it tightly enough to hold but not tightly enough to choke her. She never made any attempt to protest or struggle. It was clear that she was used to being lead by humans so this was nothing new to her.

I had the knot almost perfect when I heard something very large approaching me from behind. I heard heavy breathing and hooves stomping furrows into the earth. I could almost feel the icy breath of the animal blowing against my back, whipping at the hair on my head like a foul-smelling wind.

I didn't want to turn around. I knew exactly what was waiting for me. Nevertheless I summoned the resolve to crane my neck, albeit slowly, to look over my shoulder. I found myself face to face with almost 1,500lbs of pissed off Brahma bull, eyes rimmed with red and a mouth open and slobbering with foamy saliva. The bull was only a few feet away from me, those hooves pawing at the dirt over and over again. I swallowed deeply, my body momentarily frozen as I desperately tried to plan my next move.

It was going to charge. I could see that much in the eyes of the beast and the hunched positioning of those powerful shoulders. My reflexes would have to be fast and perfect if I didn't want to get the absolute shit gored out of me in this barren field. It seemed like we were having a staring contest, the bull and I...locked in a battle of wills. The night was silent and nothing stirred. Time stood still as I slowly turned my body to face the bull, my heels digging into the ground to gain purchase. I felt a fat bead of sweat running down my temple but I didn't dare reach up to wipe it away.

Suddenly a sound started way back in the bull's throat, a rising bellow that pierced the sanctity of the night and broke my paralysis. He was coming. Horns lowered and head bucking from side to side, he aimed himself at my torso. His charge was deceptively fast, my reaction time not nearly up to par with the speed of his approach.

I darted to my right, arms pulling close to my body to avoid the huge animal. I was quick, but not quick enough. One of the horns dug a shallow groove into my bicep, cutting straight through the material of my coat. The cut wasn't deep, but still the pain awoke me, the little droplets of blood starting to trickle down my arm. I shook it off as best I could and wheeled back around to see the bull doing the same, preparing for his next charge.

He came at me again, all bad intentions and bellowing fury. I might not get lucky this time. It was time to utilize my insurance policy...

Just as the bull was still several yards away I reached deeply into the pockets of my coat and pulled out two heavy chunks of hay, proceeding to throw them directly in the bull's direction. It had the exact reaction I was hoping for. From behind me the herd of cows suddenly all began trudging past me towards the hay, mooing and excited for the late night snack. More and more of the herd passed me in an effort to get to the hay, creating a wall of bovine flesh between myself and the bull. He was furious on the other side of that wall, stomping the dirt and snorting as he struggled to find a way to get to me.

I had no plans to stick around though.

I took the opening this distraction provided and I wrapped my hand around the rope on the old cow's neck, turning to head for the little stretch of woods beyond the field. The cow followed obediently, her old fat body swaying from side to side as she struggled to keep up with my pace.

We crossed into the underbrush and continued through the little path I had beaten through the trees. There was a little stretch of barbwire fence that I'd broken through during my trip out here and we passed by it easily. I felt a rush of adrenaline pulsing through my body, the hot little pain in my arm already forgotten. I had my quarry. I had what M wanted...

I couldn't help but laugh as I lead the old cow deeper into the woods. It was a frantic, relief-laced laugh. I detected the slightest edge of lunacy in it...and that worried me greatly.

My laughter was greeted by the distant bellow of the bull from somewhere far behind us.

Chapter 29

Roman

I walked her through that little stretch of woods and she came without ever questioning the fate that might await her. She trusted me, this old cow. She lowed and she plodded forward and at one point she even reached out with her rough tongue to lick the side of my hand. That had a bigger effect on me than I ever could have expected. The panicked amusement I felt after fleeing the field had departed.

It was being replaced by guilt, the weight of that guilt becoming heavier with each step we took towards the root cellar. I kept telling myself that there was no other way. If I defied M now it would undoubtedly mark the end of our "covenant"...and a part of me knew that it might mark the end of me and everything I cherished as well. There was too much to risk. I'd promised to do this. It was my cross to bear.

She was just a cow. Sooner or later she'd be killed and eaten anyway. The only difference here was that she'd be devoured in the darkness of the root cellar instead of at the local McDonalds. It was her destiny. She was born a cow and she was preordained to meet this kind of end. Hopefully it would be quick. At the very least, it would be honest.

That didn't make it any less hard. Seeing those rheumy eyes of hers looking at me, seeming inquisitive. Almost like she was asking me "who are we going to visit?" She was a living, breathing animal now...not just burger meat on my plate. That made it much more personal than I wanted it to be. I stroked her wet nose, trying to give her a little comfort in these last moments.

We're going to visit death, old girl.

That's where this journey ends.

The swampy overgrowth was closing in. I fought through brambles and ragged branches. The old girl's hooves splashed through little pools of stagnant water. I pushed aside a curtain of dying willow leaves and saw that we had reached our destination. The door of the root cellar loomed ahead, looking both ominous and hungry, much like the being that dwelt below.

The door was small and I was hoping the cow would fit through the opening. My concern was her width not passing through the threshold. The last thing I needed was for her to get stuck in the doorframe. I got close now, pulling on the rope while reaching out for the door...and for the first time the old cow showed signs of trepidation. She struggled a bit, lowing sadly from deep within her throat.

It was almost like she sensed the wrongness behind that door. That keen animal intuition kicking in, telling her that something horrible waited for her in there. I never thought the moo of a cow could affect me on an emotional level, but hearing the old animal make that kind of sound damn near broke my heart. It sounded far too close to human pleading for my liking...

I reached out again, my hand stroking her nose. She calmed a little, those big, milky eyes staring up at me. Her breath came out in little panicked gasps against the flesh of my hand. My voice came out in a whisper, a poor attempt to soothe the fear awakening within her.

"I'm sorry, old girl."

I started to lead her again, proceeding to push the door open with my free hand. She came willingly enough, but her legs seemed almost to tremble. She lowered her head to clear through the frame, and as I worried her sides scraped deeply against the sides of the doorframe. There was one stressful moment when I was sure she was stuck, but she managed to finally squeeze the entirety of herself into the root cellar.

I noted that a rusted nail had dug a little groove into her flank, the blood droplets already starting to drip down against the earth. She was lowing again now, the same sad, hopeless note escaping from her throat.

I closed the door behind us.

The air was thick and suffocating in here. The hole awaited us, gaping and expectant. I could feel the other presence there immediately, the vibrations in the earth indicating that something gargantuan was crawling and slithering towards the surface.

M was waiting.

M was watching.

M was coming up to feed.

Chapter 30

Roman

Little clouds of dust puffed up from the hole. A hideous scratching sound invaded my ears, causing the cow to lose control of her bowels and leave a steaming pile of shit next to my feet. I barely noticed. All of my attention was focused on the chasm in the earth. I'd forgotten to breathe. I didn't dare blink.

M was coming...and I was mortified at the thought of actually seeing him.

All motion in the root cellar abruptly came to a halt. The sound of ragged claws digging through the soil abated. The quiet seemed to pierce through me like little sharp blades digging into my perspiring skin. I could see into the hole but there was still nothing to be glimpsed except for yawning darkness. M was down in that darkness somewhere though. I could sense him just beyond the scope of my vision lurking along those earthen walls. He was close. Dangerously close.

"She's lovely, Roman. Good choice..."

M's voice echoed up from the deep, and it was the darkest purr I'd ever heard come forth from whatever M had for vocal cords. The sound of that voice made me want to swoon and drift through the warm waters of the eternal. M's pleasure was contagious and I could literally feel it infecting me.

"Bring me what is mine."

I was complying with that request without even thinking about it. The cow came easily and without any kind of struggle. There was a glaze over her eyes, a dumbfounded look. It seemed M was having the same hypnotizing effect on her as he was on me. She walked so willingly towards her ruin...

I brought her to the very edge of the pit, her hooves pushing against little crumbs of dirt and causing them to fall down into it. She stared down into that abyss, a rivulet of drool dripping from her open mouth like slow molasses.

"That's perfect. The next part is crucial, child of flesh and sinew. Listen well."

I was listening, full of tranquility and letting that purr sink into every fiber of my being.

"I'll be coming up to take her. I'll be squeezing a section of myself up into the world of the surface. I'd prefer it if you didn't see me, Roman. Not yet, anyways."

A brief pause, the cow still drooling down into the hole.

"I'm a little shy."

I found myself nodding my head. I barely even realized I was doing it.

"I'd like for you to turn around and step into that far corner. Keep your back to the hole and close your eyes. You'll count down from ten...and then it will be over. A short feast and that will be all."

I stepped towards the corner, letting the rope slip from my fingers. The cow was left there all alone with only the monstrous unknown to keep her company. I took a deep breath...and I closed my eyes. I didn't know what to expect. I had no idea what was coming. I had no time to prepare for what happened next...

That sound came again, intensifying...something of great size digging and scratching and clawing against the earth. My lips were moving in a silent whisper.

"Ten."

Dust was sprinkling down into my hair. The earthen floor was shaking violently. A stench hit my nostrils and almost knocked me to my knees. It was the odor of some deadened thing buried for centuries and being exhumed.

"Nine."

The cow's false calm had dissipated. She was not calm now. She was bellowing and the terror conveyed through those bellows made the hair stand up on the back of my neck.

"Eight."

Something was pushing upward out of the pit. My eyes remained closed but I could feel it behind me, a darkening of the root cellar. The shadow of eternity washed over me and it was so very cold in the shade of it, my blood seeming to turn icy in my veins.

"Seven."

I was trembling now. I felt silent tears washing down my cheeks. I felt my heart hammering in my chest to the point where I thought it might burst straight through the ribcage. I could hear mounds of dirt falling off of a section of M's unearthed body.

"Six."

I didn't know cows could scream. That's the only way I can describe the sound that came next, drilling into my ears. It sounded like the bovine was destroying its own throat just by making that kind of sound. The sounds that followed were even worse. I heard flesh tearing like paper. I heard sinew snapping and bones cracking. I heard wet splashing sounds and teeth so incomprehensibly large chewing and chewing and chewing...

"Five."

I heard a strange chattering like mandibles clicking together. I heard rattling and hissing and a lengthy slurping noise that threatened to make my entire skull explode. I was dimly aware of the fact that liquid was splashing around the root cellar at an alarming rate. My clothes were soaked, the liquid dripping down my back.

"Four."

Pieces of that animal were hitting the walls. Wet, fleshy chunks smacking against the confines of the root cellar. It was being eviscerated. It was being torn asunder. Blood was hitting the ceiling and then falling back downward like scarlet rain.

"Three."

I never should have opened my eyes. It was one of the worst decisions I ever made. I didn't turn around, merely opened my eyes to little slits and looked at the wall. I saw only the shadow of M. Only a portion of his shadow...but it was more than enough. I saw freakishly long limbs that ended in thin fingers with ragged fingernails the size of railroad spikes. I saw teeth that seemed to spin like a circular saw. I saw masses of skin and tumor lumps and sacs of exposed organ meat drooping low and I saw all of these things simply through the shadow cast across the walls.

I closed my eyes once again and felt the warm piss dripping down my thighs as my bladder betrayed me.

"Two."

Swallowing. The remnants of the bovine were being swallowed. The bones were being sucked of marrow. Tongues were lapping up blood. Too many tongues to understand. Too many tongues...

"One."

The dirt was moving again. The soil was shaking and grinding as M descended back into his familiar prison. His voice returned to me, gurgling and satiated.

"I've cleaned my plate. You can open your eyes now, Roman."

I did as I was bid.

I opened my eyes to an abattoir.

The walls of the root cellar were splattered with gore. Hot blood dripped from the ceiling, the coppery smell of it still fresh. I took a step backwards and squelched down against a chunk of liver. I was soaked in the remnants of that old cow. I was splashed in bile and the little pieces of shit that remained in the animal's stomach before it was consumed.

I turned to the hole, already starting to hyperventilate. The mouth of the pit was even worse. Loops of intestine trailed down into the deep. A severed leg overhung the edge, the hoof dug into the dirt like in the final moments the cow had tried in vain to pull itself back up to the surface.

The world was turning gray all around me. My vision was dimming. All the strength went out of my knees and I dropped down against the dirt. Consciousness was fading. I looked down at my own hands, grimed with blackish blood. I fell directly on my face, puffing out air against the dust.

I dove towards peaceful nothingness and away from this blood-smeared reality. I swam deeper and deeper into the darkness. I kicked my feet to escape the nightmare of it all...

The whole world fell away as I fainted. I was so thankful for that.

Chapter 31

Roman

Partial consciousness found me sometime later. My vision was bleary and nothing was tangible. I tasted dirt in my mouth. My eyelids were practically glued together with dried cattle blood. The darkness was still close and I knew it wasn't done with me just yet.

Something was singing to me. It was the softest, darkest lullaby I've ever heard in my entire lifetime. I couldn't understand the lyrics. I didn't even know if the ululations of that lullaby could be described as actual words or not. It was voiced in a language I knew nothing about, spoken in a tongue older than anything I've ever known. It was pulling me back down into the gray world of nothingness. I was content to go back there again.

I felt my hair being stroked away from my sweaty brow. I caught the barest glimpse of thin fingers that ended in jagged fingernails. It looked like there was fossil sediment encrusted beneath those fingernails. Ancient earth.

I was lost in the lullaby, being stroked like a little baby fresh out of the womb. That's what I felt like, covered in blood and meat gristle. I'd been born again into a life now scarred by hellish memories. The long fingers kept brushing through my hair. The smell of them made me want to gag.

The lullaby stopped for a moment. M whispered into my ear from somewhere behind me.

"Your kin will prosper."

I said nothing. I didn't know what to say. I couldn't find the strength to even open my mouth. It seemed too difficult a task...

"Sleep deep...rest long."

I wanted to sleep. More than anything I wanted that. The lullaby began again and I let the strange melodies carry me away. Nothing mattered but the nothingness.

I slept.

I slept deep.

Chapter 32

Roman

I don't know how long I slept. I awoke alone, M's presence somewhere down in the deep now that he'd been momentarily satiated. Dawn was breaking when I finally staggered out of the root cellar and into the harsh light of a newborn sun. I shielded my eyes against that light. I didn't want to be illuminated; I didn't want any part of my disgusting, blood-drenched form to be exposed right now.

Somehow I made it back into the house and went directly to the bathroom. My folks were still asleep and I was incredibly thankful for that. I locked the door and just leaned up against it for a moment, trying to get my breath back.

I didn't want to look in the mirror but I had a grating compulsion to do so. I slowly approached my own reflection, my eyes reluctantly taking in my own face. I looked like I had been bathed in blood and painted crimson. Little chunks of sour meat were stuck in my hair. My clothes were saturated and smeared in dirt. There was so much grime beneath my fingernails that I didn't think I'd ever be able to dig it out. I abhorred the sight of myself. I looked like a deranged murderer back from a night of endless butchery.

I peeled the clothes off and it was like peeling off actual skin, the layers so gummy and sticky against my flesh. I made a mental note to dispose of them later. I was certain no amount of laundering would remove the stain or the stink of them...

I turned the shower on, blasting the hot water as much as I could possibly stand it before stepping in. I washed and I scrubbed and I tried so hard to become clean again. I lost track of time in that shower, my skin pruning up and becoming like mush. I scrubbed the soap so hard against my skin that it was becoming painful. I just had to get clean...I had to wash the previous night away and bleach these fuckin' memories right out of my mind too.

By the time I finally stepped out and toweled off I felt mentally and physically gutted. I was raw and drained and I needed actual restful sleep more than anything else. I was afraid of closing my eyes though...

It seemed like every time I blinked the darkness showed me that abattoir again. Scenes played behind my eyelids. I heard the sounds of death; saw the mutilated bits of that cow flying all around me, the blood baptizing me in foulness...and worst of all, the sound of M going about his gluttony.

I slogged into my bedroom and I pulled a pack of Nyquil caps out of the cabinet, proceeding to pop several of them into my mouth one after another. Not enough to do any harm but enough to send me down into a dark abyss. Hopefully a dreamless abyss...

I stumbled and fell face first into my bed, naked and exhausted.

I drew the blankets up and pulled them close all around me, creating a cocoon to curl myself into.

My eyelids felt heavy and I was happy to give in to the weight of them.

The last sight I saw before drifting off again was that there was still dirt beneath my fingernails.

Still dirty.

Still unclean.

Chapter 33

Roman

The next few days passed in a haze. I felt like a zombie staggering through a fog enshrouded world, everything coming to me from a great distance away. I found myself staring blankly ahead while people attempted to engage me in conversation. I barely had any kind of appetite. I felt as weak as a kitten and even holding that valuable ruby hidden away in my room couldn't bring me back to life again.

My memories from those few days lack clarity, but several very important things happened. There were certain pivotal events that broke through the haze and hit me hard. One of them was the night my father came home and sat down at the dinner table with a conflicted look on his face. It was hard to read that expression but it looked like a mixture of happiness undercut with grief.

My mom had to work hard to get him to finally give us the news. I lost all interest in my plate of macaroni and cheese when my father finally spoke.

"Davis had a heart attack last night. He couldn't get to the phone in time...we found him laid out by the jukebox this morning."

Braham wiped a calloused hand against his lips before continuing.

"He's dead, Helena."

My mother's mouth fell open and they went through a little back and forth exchange about the death of my dad's boss. I didn't pay attention to much of it. The only word that mattered to me at that particular moment was "dead."

"Here's the craziest thing though, he made a last minute change to his will a few nights prior. I've been running it through my head over and over again and I just can't understand it."

I pushed my plate away, all of my attention focused on Braham's bearded face.

"He named me as his primary beneficiary. I ain't the janitor down there anymore..."

All was quiet in our little kitchen, my father's eyes lighting up just a bit, enough to tell us this was life-changing news.

"I own the whole damn bar."

The hugs followed. Tears flowed. Surprise and happiness spread through the kitchen and hung over my folks like a warm, fluffy cloud. Only I saw the poison hidden within that cloud. Only I recognized the darkness hiding behind the light.

I couldn't speak up about it though. My parents deserved this happiness. I'd have to swallow down this black, ugly secret and keep it locked away deep inside of me. That was the only option right now...

I thought that would be the end of it. I was wrong. A day later my mom mentioned that her muscle spasms were coming less and less frequently. A day after that she held her head perfectly high without any of the little tics that dystonia usually caused. She walked better than she had in years. She went to her neurologist and he was baffled by her condition. He'd never seen this kind of improvement in a dystonia patient in all of his time in the field.

He even used the word miracle to describe my mom's improvement.

There were more tears, more hugs, and the happiness surrounding my family only grew. Helena's pain was dissipating with each passing day. Braham finally had the career that he deserved. Everything seemed to be falling perfectly into place.

All of this had a price, though. No miracles here. God had no part in this work. These were the hands of M reaching up from the deep, many dirt-stained fingers from many long arms weaving together the things he had promised me.

He said my kin would prosper.

Through whatever dark powers he possessed, my kin *were* prospering.

The idea that M had this much influence over events occurring on the "surface" worried me greatly. It made me wonder just what else he might be capable of...

Most of all I worried about what he'd ask of me next

Chapter 34

Roman

I wanted to avoid the root cellar. It was the absolute last place in the world I wanted to visit right now. Even the promise of endless riches wasn't enough to get me back down there. Something had changed within me when M took the cow. It finally dawned on me that I was dealing with a malevolence that surpassed all rational understanding. This was not a restless spirit seeking atonement. This wasn't something I could even begin to wrap my head around.

M was the great unknown, a thing locked away in the dark depths below for longer than I'd even hazard to guess. M was voracious. M was manipulative. Above all else though, M wanted out. I was the key to that freedom. I was the skeleton key made up of flesh and sinew, the one man who could open the doorway of M's prison of soil.

Perhaps that's why M hasn't destroyed me already. He needs me. His reach can only go so far beyond the confines of that root cellar, and if he doesn't have someone to dig, someone to fetch him his supper...then he is lost. He needs a proxy to carry out his work on the surface. I remember M saying that it had been many years since someone had visited him last when I first stumbled across the crack in the earth. That was important. If there is no proxy then maybe M is powerless. Maybe he can only watch and wait and hope that someone else will come along and find him down there in the dirt.

I might still have a chance to end this before it gets worse.

I was feeling the pull. I knew he wanted me to visit soon. I would go. I had no choice but to go. It wasn't the promises that commanded me now, it was the veiled threats. I'd experienced exactly what kind of damage M could do to mold a better life for me and mine. I'd hate to see what he could do if he wanted to bring the whole world crashing down on top of us. Something tells me that M is an expert in the art of human suffering.

It was extremely hard to deny him but I knew deep down that it wasn't impossible. M could be resisted. If the willpower is there, M can even be defied.

It's just a matter of facing up to the consequences that follow that defiance. I found myself thinking about those dreams again. The corpse in the dirty brown suit was trying to tell me something. Somehow he was connected to all of this. He was trying to reach me from beyond the grave, from behind the curtain of death...to tell me to stop digging. Stop feeding the beast. Stop all of this before it's far too late.

I'd made my decision.

I would return to M tonight.

I cannot be a slave to this abomination anymore. I cannot wear these invisible shackles because my wrists are tearing and my mind is shattering. I have to find a way to end this. I must break this covenant; I must turn away from this hole full of promises.

M and I have one thing in common.

We both want to be free.

Chapter 35

Roman

I matched my breathing to each step, inhale and pause, exhale and move forward. I filled my lungs with icy night air and then spat it back out again in nervous gasps. My hand was on the door of the root cellar, just resting there. I was tracing across the pitted surface of the wood, letting my fingernails drag a bit. I was stalling, trying in vain to put off the inevitable.

I could sense M lurking in the hole beyond that door. I knew before even entering that he was alert and waiting. I even got the strong feeling that he'd become incredibly impatient with me.

I opened the door. I passed through the threshold, the cobwebs catching in my hair, the splinters from the doorframe falling down against my shoulders like shredded snowflakes. I sniffed the air and almost choked on it, the drying blood and clotted bits of meat still littering M's lair from his last feeding.

I barely took a step forward before something like invisible hands took hold of me and propelled me forward like a human doll, the toes of my shoes dragging against the earth as I was literally *pulled* towards the gaping hole in the center of the root cellar. This was something new. Something I hadn't expected, a wholly awful sensation. I dangled a few inches like a marionette over the edge of the abyss, gazing down into the darkened burrows of M's prison.

I could still move my limbs, but M had me in his grasp regardless. It was like he was utilizing some form of telekinesis, just strong enough to keep me from placing my heels back down onto the ground.

So I hovered, helpless and at the mercy of the monster in the chasm. My eyes rolled in my head and took in the gore-decorated walls of this hidden, lonely place. This was a bad place to die. Not a place where the dead would be allowed to rest. I didn't want to die here. Anywhere but here...

"I'm not a big fan of waiting, Roman. I've been waiting for centuries and it's taken a bit of a toll on my patience. You understand that, don't you?"

M's voice washed over me, forcing little cold drops of sweat to burst out of almost every visible pore.

"Everyone should have priorities in life. I am your priority, child of flesh and sinew. I am the first thing you should think about when you wake and the last thing you should think about when you sleep. I am your full time job. I am your life."

M's voice changes in tone, becoming like thunder from the bowels of the earth, dust rattling and puffing up from below. The unseen grip on me tightens, my body starting to spasm just a bit.

"I am the reason you take breath into your fucking mouth and I am the reason that you are not a pile of blood and shit squashed into this dirt. You exist because I let you. You exist to SERVE. Say it with me, kiddo! I...exist...to serve."

My mouth is moving against my will, my lips trembling, my vocal cords forming words that fall out like sharp little razorblades against the tip of my tongue.

"I exist to serve, M."

"Glad we've established that! Keep me waiting again, Roman...and you will die slow. You will die knowing that your family is rotting. I will fuck up your entire little world, and I will do it with ease because you are like an aphid to me. That is all your life amounts to when compared to my own."

I feel something like a needle pointed blade digging down across my throat, not enough to pierce flesh but enough to sting and drive M's point even deeper.

"All life screams when it's being digested in the juices of my stomachs, Roman. If you go to that dark, wet place...you will scream too, loudest of all. Remember that."

The unseen hands vanished and suddenly my body was my own again. My feet dropped back to the floor and I began wheeling my arms for balance dangerously close to the edge of the pit. Finally I gained it, stepping back and breathing deeply, trying hard to swallow back the fear.

I was afraid, there was no denying that. But I was also angry. I felt that anger throbbing in the back of my head and threatening to burst out of my skull.

"What more do you want from me?" I asked, my fists clenching at my sides.

"The million dollar question! Here's the thing, Roman. I'm starting to get my strength back, starting to finally feel like my old self again. I need meat to keep that process moving forward. Think of it as fuel for the machine. I have powers that your little monkey mind wouldn't even be able to comprehend...but they all have their price. I need to take in sustenance if I want to expend energy. The stronger I become, the more sustenance I need."

My fingernails were biting down into the flesh of my palms, my fists becoming tighter and tighter. I focused on that pain. I gathered my rage into the little rivets that were forming there.

"I expended quite a bit of energy getting your daddy that promotion and sucking some of the sickness out of your mommy. That energy needs to be replaced. The machine needs fuel. The bovine was enough to get me going again, but it's not what something like me really needs. I have very specific tastes."

"Something bigger than the cow? Sorry to break it to you, M, but I don't think I'll be able to get my hands on an elephant here in West Virginia. Rust Valley isn't really their natural habitat..." I surprised myself, the sarcastic venom in my voice unmistakable. M responded with a gurgling little titter.

"Such spirit! That's why I like you, child of flesh and sinew. Laughter feeds the soul just as meat feeds the belly. It's not a larger beast that I'm craving. It's a beast higher up on the evolutionary chain. They walk on two legs, drive metal tubes with wheels, reproduce constantly and taste a little like broiled pork."

My eyes widened, my nostrils flared. I knew where M was going with this but just hearing it aloud seemed to make it all the more real.

"Maybe you've heard of them before? They're called human beings. Delicious little parasites that are abundant in numbers. That's what I'm hungry for. That's what I need to put the pep into my step again! Just one will suffice to start. Only one, Roman...you'll just need to bring me one..."

My face was a portrait of horrors. I was already stepping back from the hole, slowly and carefully.

"You are asking me...to bring you a person?"

I struggled to even get the words out. The anger was back again, racing through my veins and hardening my expression. My jaw was set, my muscles becoming like steel beneath my skin.

"I won't do that."

This didn't seem enough, so I strove to hammer the point home even more.

"I will *never* do that."

M was coming now. The ground was shaking and the dust was pluming and I heard those hideous scrabbling sounds on the walls of the burrow. I could feel his rage ascending with him. It was caustic and hot, acid in the air around me. Those unseen hands settled across me again, struggling to hold me in place.

I reached deep down into myself, into the iron in my guts and whatever courage I had to draw from...and I fought those invisible bands clamping against my limbs. I fought them hard. I felt them first loosening, and then falling away completely. I felt M's surprise when I managed to do that. His ascent was halted for just a moment. I imagined him shocked down there in the hole, in complete disbelief that I had that much fight in me.

I was already turning to run for the door. M was ascending again, much faster than before, the walls rattling all around me. I dove for the door just as dirt exploded up into the air from behind me, that horribly twisted shadow falling across me and darkening everything in the root cellar.

I sensed multiple hands scraping and seeking across the dirt.

One of those hands even brushed against the back of my boot before I threw open the door and slammed it closed behind me. I kept running until my lungs felt like they were full of fire. I didn't stop until I'd reached the old Buick parked in front of the house.

I had escaped. I was alive and still breathing.

I was free.

Chapter 36

Roman

I found myself behind the wheel of the Buick and tearing out of the driveway, bits of gravel flying out behind the tires as I hammered down on the gas pedal. I just needed to drive as far away from M's lair as possible. I needed time to think, time to plan my next step. I'd defied him. I'd blatantly told him no, and I even managed to resist the beguiling pull of his presence. Consequences would be coming.

I can't let this thing destroy my family. I have to find a way to stop him. Just like the dead man in the dirty brown suit said, it was time to bury M deep and salt the earth. Could I do that? Could I seal up that root cellar and fill that hole in forever? M told me himself that he's lacking on energy and needs to refuel. He might only have a little power left in the tank. If ever he was weak, it was now. The fact that I'd managed to escape him proved that to me. This was my opportunity, and if I missed it now, it might not come round again.

I drive down lonely mountain roads, the forest encroaching on either side of the cracked asphalt. My headlights pierce through the darkness ahead. I keep one hand on the wheel and the other I use to massage my temple. I don't bother with the radio, music won't help right now. I need silence. I need to figure this out.

If I close M's opening to the surface I think it's highly possible that he'll be defeated. That is his window into the world of mankind. He works his machinations from the depths of that hole and if that hole is blocked off, his passage is severed. No more proxies. No more food. Nothing but the blackness and the worms to keep M company down there.

I'd need heavy machinery to do it, probably an excavator. My dad used to work general labor for a construction company in the outskirts of Rust Valley so I knew the perfect place to rent one. I still had enough money to do that, and if all else fails I still have that ruby socked away too. I'd tell the operator that we're remodeling the house and we want that root cellar buried and rolled over, obliterated into nothing but forgotten dirt and lost whispers in the ground.

It's still early, maybe the foreman will still be at the field office if I get there quick. This is my glimmer of hope. This is the pathway to lasting freedom, not the panicked respite that I've been granted now. A happy ending might not be too far out of reach after all...

These are the thoughts that circle through my head as the deer crosses in front of the Buick. I have enough time to notice that it's a young six-point buck. It stands there, frozen in place, eyes seeming glazed over and unseeing. The headlights illuminate everything, like the buck is the star of the show and he's standing in his very own spotlight on a cracked asphalt stage. In these precious moments before everything goes to shit, I see the buck in incredibly vivid detail. The inky eyes, the soft fur, the planted hooves. Something is off about the deer though. There's a spindly little thing perched on the tip of one antler. I squint even as I'm struggling to turn the wheel and swerve.

It's a house centipede.

Possibly the same one I shook from my hand when I went down to get the candles in the root cellar seemingly a lifetime ago. It regards me with many eyes, seems almost to wave at me with numerous twitching legs. The strangest thing about it is that the little insectivore seems almost to be mocking me in those final moments.

I'm pulling at the wheel so hard my arms are becoming sore. The tires screech and the stink of burnt rubber fills my nostrils. The bumper clips the deer's hindquarters and the animal is flung out of my view. I feel suddenly weightless and I don't understand why at first. It's because gravity has turned upside down as the car flips and rolls in midair, the seatbelt biting deeply into my torso.

I see sparks. Something splashes my thigh and I realize it's water from the radiator. I'm locked in a womb of twisting metal and the first time my head hits the steering wheel I see stars, the second time I see those same stars fading.

There is so much sound in my ears, pounding at my skull. Something sharp has stabbed into my shoulder and I feel my own hot blood pouring down from the wound. That side of my body feels like a sack filled with broken things that can never be fixed again. I'm spinning and my stomach is churning and a vague sense of gravity returns to me.

I am falling, strapped in my seatbelt and embraced by the ruined metal of something that used to be my vehicle. The front of the car crunches down against the asphalt and I have time to notice the engine smashing up through the dashboard. The windshield explodes, showering me with little glass raindrops.

One final thought comes to me then. I know M did this.

And then my world is all white and blistering and I know nothing more.

Part II: Unearthed

Chapter 37

Thorny Rose

There is only lamplight in my room. It is dim here and darkness tends to reign. I like the shadows. I feel safe in the shadows. The objects of my obsession look down at me from framed posters on the walls. Jeffrey Dahmer, John Wayne Gacy, Charles Manson, Albert Fish. They watch me as I sleep; my collection of serial killers with many pairs of curiously deadened eyes. I love to read about them. I love to learn about them. I lie on my bed and I twirl strands of my black hair around my finger as I read about cannibalism and mutilation and the soulless crimes of those special few who crossed the boundaries into the land of taboo.

My hand reaches out to grab my phone, the chipped black nail polish looking like tendrils of corruption, bits of it starting to flake off. I'd need a fresh coat soon. I touch the screen and I'm greeted with a familiar sight. Nothing. No text messages, no Facebook comments, no likes on my Instagram pictures. It's like I'm the only living person in a world of ghosts, never noticed in my offline life or my online life either. Or perhaps I'm the ghost and the living ignore me because they don't even realize I'm here. Sometimes it feels that way, like I'm flitting through an abysmal world where nothing really matters and the only destination in sight is a pit filled with swirling blackness and dying motivation.

There are no texts from Roman. There are never any texts from Roman. That cuts deeper than the straight razor ever does when I let it kiss my flesh. Does he even have the slightest clue how I feel about him? Probably not. I'm little more than a passing acquaintance, an extra that occasionally makes an appearance in the screenplay of Ro's life. I never have many lines in that screenplay. I'm just background noise, the oddball in black with a secret crush that weighs her down and threatens to turn her heart into a blazing inferno.

Ro with his dark hair and thoughtful eyes. I'd like to kiss him and never stop. I'd like to feel his chest beneath my hands. I'd like to bite into his lip and draw just a few rubies of blood, just a taste, you know? Nothing bad. I just want to take in a little part of him so that we'll always be together. United, like a knot that not even the most skillful fingers can undo. Maybe I'm a broken doll with a few mental cracks, but porcelain can be mended. Ro could do that for me. I believe that in the deepest recesses of my soul.

I roll from my bed and I crawl over to the full length mirror along the wall. My movements are languid, much like the slither of snake waking from hibernation. The mirror is shattered in multiple places. Many fist-sized indentations mark the surface of the glass, showing me so many different little reflections. I hate all of those little reflections, each and every one of them.

I try to smile, my lips curving and my teeth showing. I examine my own smile in the shattered mirror. It's the grin of something alien attempting to mimic normal human emotion. It's unusual and it inspires such a loathing in me. I cannot explain this. It's always been this way.

Somewhere beyond the paper thin walls of this room, my mother is screaming my name. Her voice is hoarse, choked and warped by decades of chain smoking. She wants her pills. She wants me to bring her pain pills. Her fucking pills. Her goddamn motherfucking pills. She wants them. She needs them. Where are they, Rose? Where are they, you little *bitch*?

I take the special cedar box out from underneath my bed. I open it and take out the prize within. It's my straight razor, stainless steel blade so keenly sharp with a carved ivory handle. It's very nice. The craftsmanship is exceptional.

I pull back my shawl and expose my arms. The scars crisscross the pallid texture of my flesh like roadmaps leading to entirely new states of pain. Some of the scars are very old and others are new, still scabby and irritated. My eyes narrow to slits as the blade sinks in, that familiar sensation settling into this poor excuse for a husk that is my body. My eyes narrow to slits. My breathing becomes shallow. The sound of blood slowly dripping is soothing, pitter-patter it goes, kind of like a lullaby.

I cut long and I cut deep. I give it lots of attention. I try so very hard to cut out all the ugliness, but it always grows back. The petals of this Rose are meant to last, and the thorns can only do so much.

Chapter 38

Thorny Rose

I have a secret name for my mother. I'm good at keeping secrets. I have many of them. I do not think of her as mother, or mom, or mama. I do not associate her birth name with her either. It's Rebecca, very mundane. The name I've labeled my mother with in my mind is Filth. She earns this title. She is a repulsive human being on the inside and outside. I think somewhere along the way the squalor she lives in started to infect her soul, eating away at it and making it equally dirty and foul.

I'm standing above her now, my hand outstretched with a few of her Oxycontin pills in my hand. It gives me time to study her. She has the face of a shrunken apple, tiny rotten crisps lining her mouth where teeth once were. They are all gone now; just jagged fragments of brown enamel remain, jutting up out of the gums like miniature spikes. Her eyes are always bloodshot and watching.

Her recliner is nestled into one of the only clear sections of the living room, bordered on all sides by stacks and stacks of junk that make up the hoard my mother has collected from yard sales and flea markets over the years. She feels comfortable in the kingdom of her hoard, a little rat queen with twitching cheeks and yellowing fingernails. She is watching television. She's almost always watching television. She likes survivalist shows best, the ones that show men and women struggling to endure the unforgiving harshness of nature. She delights in watching the suffering of others, even if it's just moving pictures flashing across a screen.

She takes the pills from my hand, those fingernails dragging against my palm just enough to hurt. It's always intentional with Filth. Nothing is accidental.

She stinks of human shit. Sometimes she shits herself in the chair and wallows in it for awhile. She makes me clean the chair when she finally goes to bed on the ragged old mattress nestled further back in the maze of the hoard. It's just one of her little games. It's designed to humiliate me, to keep me subservient.

I fantasize about killing her almost every single day. I invent entirely new and innovative ways to do it. Maybe I could push down one of the heavy stacks while she's in the chair and crush her beneath the avalanche of nicknacks. Maybe I could grab her by the thinning hair of her ponytail and slam dunk her head through the screen of the television. Maybe I can use my teeth tear through the loose, filth-encrusted skin that covers the bluish veins of her throat.

I fantasize about lots of things.

"Been pricking yourself again, Rosie? Those look fresh."

I pull the black sleeve of my sweater just a little bit farther down to cover up the lacerations on my forearm. I hate when she calls me Rosie. She knows that I hate it. She makes it a point to call me Rosie every single time I'm forced to interact with her. Filth is very good at her little games. She has nothing but time to create new ones and sit on her ass all day while collecting worker's compensation ever since she threw her back out stocking shelves at Food Mart.

"You know, I just don't get it, Rosie. Got a roof over your head and a little tummy full of food that I buy for you, and still you gotta cut yourself up. Ain't that just the weirdest fuckin' thing?"

I do not reply. Her voice is grating and bubbly. It reminds me of sewer water gurgling up from a malfunctioning toilet.

"Ever since you slid out past my thighs I knew you were twisted up in the head, just like your Daddy was. He was all twisted up until the very day he died. Used to burn himself with cigarettes, I ever tell you that?"

Yes. She had told me that seemingly hundreds of times. I never knew my father. He died when I was only two years old. A cigarette dropped from his fingers in the little bedroom down the hall while he slept and the whole room had gone up in flames right along with Daddy. All that remained was his right foot burnt off at the ankle. The rest was ash. That room is still there, a charred ruin with the door nailed shut and blocked off from the rest of the house. It happened in less than a few hours. I guess the hoard was good tinder for the fire.

I try to change the subject.

"Is there anything left to eat tonight?" I ask, my eyes wandering over to the remnants of the frozen microwavable dinner that she has already devoured. She reaches down to pick up a little piece of chicken bone, slurping the marrow down past her warty tongue.

"There's a can of Vienna sausages in the mini fridge back there. You can have that."

The mini fridge hasn't worked in at least seven years, some type of electrical issue. Filth knows this. I once checked the expiration date on that can of Vienna sausages. They expired exactly fifteen years ago. Filth knows this too.

"I think I'll go for a walk."

I like taking long walks at night. There's one particular destination that I visit pretty often. It's a special place for me. A secret place too.

"You do that."

Filth pops the pills into her mouth and washes them down with a can of generic soda from Food Mart. She adjusts herself a bit in the chair, seeming to take careful care to rub her buttocks all around the material of the recliner's seat.

"Don't forget to scrub down my chair when you get home."

I move through the maze of the hoard and I'm out the front door, the stink of human shit fading as I take in the freshness of the cold night air.

Chapter 39

Thorny Rose

I like winter. It's December now in Rust Valley and the cold bites deeply. I'm wearing my big black coat with the hood that drapes down very low, almost obscuring my eyes. The freezing air feels good in my lungs. My breath is a spreading mist and I walk through that mist with each step forward. Cold tends to numb. I enjoy feeling numb. I imagine when you're dead, you feel numb. Just cold and empty locked away in a box hidden from everything and everyone.

Sounds nice.

I've walked this same trail many times before, usually at night. It veers off from the highway and cuts into the woods. Trees with bare arms loom above me on all sides, the undergrowth scraping against my coat as I walk. The moon is full tonight and it cuts through the scraggly canopy above and provides me with all the light that I need. If my entire life was illuminated by nothing but moonlight I think that would make me very happy. Moonlight is all I need. More than enough.

This little trail through the wilderness leads to Legion Lane. It opens to a thorny clearing with a section of trampled down barbwire fence to separate it from the road. There are only a few houses on Legion Lane, most of them far apart. One of those houses is very important to me. It's very old and time has not been kind to it. The back of the house is lost in a swampy area; almost like the very building itself is trying to return to nature. The house is not important to me. The person who lives in the house is, though.

It's Roman Merrick's house.

I come here all the time to this particular spot. I don't actually go up to the house and knock on the door or anything. That would be weird. This vantage point gives me a perfect view of his bedroom window. There is no curtain up within. The foliage and brambles lets me stand here perfectly still, hiding in plain sight. I just like to watch. There's nothing wrong with watching. It's my little window into Roman's world.

I deserve that much, don't I?

Some nights I get lucky. I've caught glimpses of him changing, pulling his undershirt up over his head and shaking out that dark, wavy hair. I can just see the tops of his bare shoulders from this angle, everything else cut off by the bottom of the window frame. That's alright. I have a vivid imagination.

During these rare, lucky moments, I reach down and rub at my crotch through the material of whatever long black skirt I'm wearing that night. I encourage the warmness that spreads down there. I tease myself until my inner thighs are sticky and I keep watching him from afar. These are our intimate moments. The cold air hardens my nipples beneath my shirt and I imagine what might happen if Roman looked out and saw me standing here. That might ruin things though. I feel closest to him when I'm just watching. There is no harm in watching.

A frown creases my lips because Roman's window is dark now. He's not home tonight. I guess his mom is asleep because the whole house is dark. I know his father works the grave shift at the American Legion downtown so he's not here either. That's discouraging. I was hoping for a Ro sighting tonight. It always lifts my spirits.

During the rare occasions when I run into him in town I try so very hard to be witty and casual around him. It takes incredible concentration to do that. It exhausts me, leaves me drained. Whenever I see him I must resist the urge to pounce and rip his shirt open and the lick the sweat off his chest. I can only really be myself when I watch him through his window. All masks cast aside, it's a cathartic feeling.

I guess it's time to walk back home now. Time to clean the scum from Filth's chair and then return to my room and then fall down into slumber. Maybe I'll cut some more of the ugliness out if the desire becomes unbearable. I'm about to turn away when something stops me dead in my tracks.

There's a soft, haunting melody coming from the back of Ro's house. I turn my head, struggling to hear it better. It's coming from somewhere near the back of the house, the area obscured by swampy growth and dead trees.

It sounds like a lullaby.

It's strange...because I hear the melody in my head just as much as I hear it in my ears. It's like a siren song beckoning me closer. Could Ro be back there somewhere? It doesn't sound anything like him. It doesn't sound like anything I've ever heard before. It is both sweet and sad, infinitely powerful.

I should leave. I should walk home now. Instead I'm walking towards the source of that lullaby. My feet are moving and they almost don't even feel like my own appendages right now. I push through the brambles and the twisted tree limbs. I have to kneel and lower my head in some places. It reminds me of the hoard maze at home. I must have stepped down into hidden water because my combat boots are soaked through. There's a door back here. I can see it in the distance beyond the dying vegetation. I do not know where it leads, but the lullaby is coming from behind that door.

Thorns cut into me as I progress towards the door that leads down into the dirt.

I barely notice.

I'm used to the thorns.

Chapter 40

Thorny Rose

I stand before gnarled wood, a little door with a little lullaby behind it. It is wide but not very high. That's okay. I'm not very tall anyways. Poison ivy curls all around the door, most of it dead and brown since we're in the early months of winter. Once when I was a little girl I rubbed poison ivy all over my privates just to see what might happen. It became very itchy down there. I scratched and scratched until my fingers were all red and wet. I touched my fingers to my lips after that and sucked all the scarlet off of them. It was a learning experience for me.

I open the door quietly and step inside. This is an earthy place. It's very dark and hard to see. I smell freshly furrowed dirt and the stinky odor of something dead and rotting. I smell blood too. I have a keen sense of smell when it comes to blood. Those smells are all on the surface, though. There is something beneath them all. It's stronger. It's the dominant scent in this dark and earthy place. I cannot place it. I cannot put a name to it. It's like pressing your nostrils against a portal that leads to the unfathomable and inhaling until you explode from within.

My eyes are finally starting to adjust to the blackness. I walk forward, exploring a bit, and immediately I have to stop myself and take a shaky step backwards. I nearly stepped over the edge of a big hole in the center of the room. It's slightly larger than a grave and it seems bottomless. How is that possible? Are my eyes betraying me again? They do that sometimes. Sometimes they show me things I'm not meant to see.

There's dried blood all around the hole. There are gristles of rotting flesh too. Looks like some kind of animal flesh. That explains the smell of decay. Is someone buried down here? Maybe it's a little cemetery reserved for one.

Everything is silent now. The lullaby is gone. Maybe it was never there at all. Sometimes there is a whisper in my head that speaks of dreadful things. It is always hushed and raspy. It always wants me to cut and slice and tear and mangle until my body is nothing but wet red ribbons. The lullaby sounded different though. I don't think it originated in my head like the whisper did.

"Hello, Rose."

I spin around, suddenly spooked. I rub at the scars along my arms like totems of protection.

"Who said that?"

I squint and slowly rotate in a circle, searching out every corner to see where that greeting came from. There's nothing. I'm alone in here.

"I'm down here."

It came from the hole. There's someone down there in the hole. I should be afraid but I'm not. I guess I feel fear just like anyone else but it's a small critter that lives in the back of my mind and it's easy to ignore. My curiosity is the larger critter in my mind and it always jumps forward and overshadows the fear.

I lean down and peer into the hole. It seems endless. I wonder where it leads. I'll be in a hole like that someday. We all end up in a hole. We all go to live with the worms. Worms are good for the environment. They eat the dead.

"I can't see you..."

"That's okay, Rose. I'm far below. You can hear me though, can't you?"

The voice seems to come from a long way away, kind of like an echo traveling through miles of cavernous space. I like the voice immediately. It sounds friendly. It sounds understanding. It talks to me like it's known me for years.

"Yes. Was that you singing just a minute ago? I heard it from outside."

Silence greets me as a response but I'm certain the voice is still there. I think maybe the voice is a bit shy and self-conscious. I can't help but smile a little. We have so much in common.

"It was beautiful."

"I'm glad you liked it. Music soothes the soul. It makes the whole world spin. It's fun to spin sometimes, Rose."

The voice is right. I like to spin. I love to twirl. I loved the merry-go-round when I was a little girl. I liked that dizzy feeling most of all. The whisper that wanted me to cut and tear always faded when I was spinning on the merry-go-round.

I'm twirling now in spite of myself, my long black skirt gathered up in my hands. I feel amazing. I feel happier than I've felt in years. There's color in my cheeks and I truly believe that I'm capable of anything right now. Finally I stop myself and return my attention to the hole.

"What's your name?"

"It's very old and very lost and your tongue would split into a thousand pieces if you were to try and speak it. You can call me what a mutual acquaintance of ours calls me, though..."

I cock my head, my black hair hanging down into my face like a veil.

"Roman calls me M."

My heart flutters. My breath quickens. These are the subtleties of obsession.

"You know Ro?"

"I do, Rose. He's my very good friend. He was working with me on a special project. I've gotten to know him very well. It's a terrible shame about the accident..."

Now my heart is leaping and crawling up my throat and threatening to suffocate me. I am being strangled by panic. I start to scratch at my scars without even realizing that I'm doing it.

"What accident? Is Roman okay?"

"It was dark and his car veered off the road. The woods of this town are crawling with deer and one strolled out in front of him at the wrong moment. The car flipped many times. It was a Buick, I think. Now it is a metal husk blackened by persistent fire. Roman is in the hospital downtown."

I'm already turning to leave. My voice feels strained and I can't even think straight. His name just keeps flashing across my thoughts like the beam of a lighthouse. Ro. Ro. Ro. Gotta get to Ro.

"I'm sorry M, I have to go now. I have to go see Ro. He'll need me. He'll want to see me."

M's voice stops me with my hand on the door. The panic starts to wash away. I'm compelled to turn back around. I feel suddenly very calm. That's strange.

"There's nothing you can do for him now, Rose. Roman is medicated and deeply asleep. I'm fairly certain he'll sleep for a long time. Comas are tricky."

A tear is running down my cheek. I feel it smearing through my black eye shadow. It feels sticky and gross and I want to wipe it away but my arm feels very heavy and I feel kind of tired too.

"No tears, sweet one. Roman is tough. He's like a stringy piece of gristle that sticks in your teeth and stays there to disturb you for weeks. Very tough. I have no doubt that he'll open his eyes to the world again very soon. I can even expedite that process, if you like..."

"You can help him wake up?"

I'm hopeful, the question sounding slurred and slow as it comes out of my mouth.

"Of course. I can do many wondrous things, Rose. I can give you the love that you crave, for example. It's not wrong to desire love. You're a charming, talented creature...and the world should love you. You deserve fame. You deserve to be adored. I'd like to see you take your rightful place as the belle of the ball, sweet one."

Something is happening now. Images are flashing across my eyes. I'm on stage at a massive rock concert. There are thousands of people in the crowd. I'm singing and playing the guitar. People are moshing and throwing up the devil horns and screaming my name over and over again. They love me. They notice me. I matter to them.

"I can make them love you, Rose. You'll be a darkly delicious queen for all of them to fantasize about. Most importantly, I can make Roman love you. It's not enough for him to just open his eyes. When he awakens, he should open his eyes and see you as the one woman that he's always wanted in his life. He should see you for the treasure that you truly are."

It's happening again. I'm seeing visions coming up from the dirt. I'm feeling Roman's hand on my cheek. I taste his lips on my own. He's holding me close and we're gazing out at the ocean on a warm summer's night.

I'm weeping openly now. I can't help it.

"I can give you his heart, Rose. All you have to do is ask."

I don't even have to think about it. My decision is made. My choice is finalized.

My path has never been clearer.

"I want it. All of it."

"That's my girl! All this talk of love and we've left out hate entirely, haven't we? It's another strong human emotion. One of the most honest, in my humble opinion. Very freeing too. I know a secret, Rose! I know who you hate..."

I know too. I'm thinking about her now. Her ugly, shrunken face. Her shit-stained chair. Her little tortures, her little games. I say her name through gritted teeth. Her true name, the one she's earned.

"Filth."

"A fitting title for such a vile monster. Bring her to me, Rose. Bring Mommy over for a visit. That's how we'll seal our deal!"

M's voice becomes low and silky, the voice of a fellow conspirator whispering to his closest ally.

"I'll take care of her for you."

I'm grinning. It's a very big grin. Sometimes I search for pictures of wolves on the internet and I think they grin in the exact same way that I'm grinning now.

Filth deserves a present. She deserves a great big surprise. I'm sure M has one for her down in that deep, dark hole.

I wipe my tears away. There's no need for them now. The future is full of promise. I've made a new friend. A special, powerful friend. I can feel that in my bones.

"It would be my pleasure, M."

I twirl a lock of my long black hair between my fingers. I do that when I'm particularly content.

"What are you, M? You're granting all these wishes for me. Are you a genie or something like that?"

M laughs. I fall in love with his laugh the moment I hear it. He's not laughing at me like all the kids at school used to do. He's not teasing me or making me feel bad. He makes me feel warm and happy. He's laughing with me instead of against me.

"Something like that."

Chapter 41

Thorny Rose

I slept so good last night after my meeting with my new friend. I awoke and stretched like a kitty cat. I was even tempted to purr. Nothing could shatter this mood. Nothing could wipe away my smile. Not even Filth as she sat there at the breakfast table slurping bacon past her rancid teeth. She didn't offer me anything. Not even one bite. Still I smiled at her.

She watched her soap operas in the afternoon. She mooned at her favorite soap actors as they romanced the damsels in distress. She greedily sucked down soda all the while and belched out from the gaseous depths of her corrupt soul. I watched the soaps with her. She offered me nothing to drink. Still I smiled at her.

Dinner came late that night. It was lasagna, extra cheesy. Filth could cook a decent meal when she actually dragged herself into the kitchen on rare occasions. I never broke eye contact with her as she shoveled the tasty meat and cheese into her mouth. Her gaze remained shrewd, but I knew her interest was piqued.

She ate every last bite and then licked her foul fingers after it was done. She offered me nothing. She preferred me thin, was fond of telling me that I could stand to lose a little weight. I can remember nights in my room where I literally thought I was starving because of her. The stomach pains, the fatigue, the agony of going to bed with nothing in your belly. It was all her doing. I smiled at her brighter than ever now.

She finally cracked.

"Well aren't you chipper today, Rosie. Why is that?"

I told her all about it. I'd been rehearsing my story in my head ever since I woke up this morning. I told her about the big garage sale happening this evening in the back of the Merrick house. Filth's eyes lit up like bloodshot lanterns. She loved yard sales, flea markets, auctions...any kind of sale that gave her the opportunity to add more useless junk to her growing hoard. It's too cold out now for yard sales so she'd been going through withdrawals. Now was the chance to feed into her compulsion.

"Just down the road there? I gotta check that out. That snooty ass Helena better have some good prices on her nicknacks. And if she don't...I'll haggle her right into the ground."

Filth grinned wide, exposing gums that looked extremely unhealthy and teeth that would give just about any dentist the nightmare of a lifetime. She was already rising to her feet and drawing her ratty old jacket tight around her shoulders. She paused only to take the leftovers that remained on her plate and dump them into the garbage disposal. She grinned at me as she did that. That renewed my hatred for her even more, adding a few more splashes of gasoline onto the inferno growing inside of me. I smiled back.

"I'll tag along." I replied, casual and perfectly composed.

Filth looked momentarily distrustful. She then shrugged her shoulders, giving me the idea that she didn't really give a shit one way or another.

"Suit yourself. I ain't buying you a damn thing though, Rosie."

She hawked up a glob of phlegm and spat it out onto the floor while shoving her wrinkly old feet into mud-encrusted work boots.

"So don't get your hopes up."

She was already halfway out the door, the sun lowering against the horizon and outlining every hideous flaw on the old monster's face. I followed behind her, making sure to pull my black hood down low against my face. I allowed myself a little smirk while her back was turned to me.

"That's alright, mama."

I caught sight of my own reflection in one of the windows. All long black hair and twinkling eyes, hooded and hateful. I didn't shy away. I think I'm starting to like my reflection now.

"I just want to spend some time with you."

Chapter 42

Thorny Rose

It wasn't hard getting her across the road. She never hesitated on the shortcut leading through the woods either. Filth had her eye on the garage sale prize right now. Her compulsion spurred her onward. She had a bloodhound's nose for sniffing out useless crap, and she thought she was on the trail. I kept pace a few feet behind her the whole way. There was no conversation. I had no last minute doubts about what I was doing.

I knew something absolutely horrible would happen to my mother when she walked into that root cellar. I didn't know exactly what, but I had a sneaking suspicion that it would be bloody and violent.

I was hoping for that.

Filth didn't even slow down when we reached that overgrown patch leading back to the door. She plodded and swatted through brambles and thorns like a stupid, stubborn mule. I made sure we approached the door from the back of the house just in case Roman's parents were home. We couldn't risk being seen. There needed to be no witnesses to this little mother and daughter stroll.

The old monster hesitated when we reached the door. Her upper lip curled back from her teeth in something akin to a dog's snarl. I couldn't help but stare at the scraggy ingrown hairs growing along the top of that lip. The dying sunlight seemed almost to catch on them.

"What the hell kinda place is this for a garage sale, Rosie?"

"It's the back entrance, mama. It leads straight through to the garage."

She responded with a grunt, seeming to accept this. I moved in front of her and slowly opened the door, gesturing for her to go first. She likes to go first in everything in life. This was no exception. Filth shoved past me and I followed behind, silently closing the door behind us and shutting out the light.

"Fuckin' dark in here. What kinda shit you pulling here, little girl?"

She wheeled around to face me, her expression pulling down into a grimace. It was like seeing a frown appear on dead apple skin. I used to be so afraid of that face when I was a little girl. There is no fear in me now, especially not for this bent, wrinkly old monster. I can only bring myself to feel one thing for her now.

Hatred. Caustic, passionate hatred.

I could feel M all around me in here. It was like he was stroking me with invisible hands, helping me to stay strong and vigilant. My confidence was as hard as stone in the presence of my new friend.

Something started to happen. Suddenly Filth began walking backwards. It was bizarre because she didn't seem to be controlling her own legs. They moved in twitchy, staggering steps. Her mouth pulled down into a hideous expression, like she was fighting some unseen force to gain back the control of her limbs.

She stopped at the very edge of the hole. Her fingers were contorting and her arms fighting to reach upwards. There was stark terror in her yellowish eyes. Her body was not her own right now. The old monster had finally met something she was powerless against. Something she wouldn't be able to intimidate or torture.

Filth seemed to be held there in place, frozen and twitching. I stepped towards her, closing the distance. Her eyes pleaded with me. Even though she was unable to speak I could easily see what she wanted. She wanted me to help her. She wanted me to save her. She wanted mercy from her little Rosie.

I stood before her, my face inches from her own. My hood cast dark shadows across my face. I could see my own eyes reflected in Filth's murky gaze. They were cold, detached. They were orbs filled with murderous intentions.

M's voice floated up from the deep. Just two simple words...but they were music to my ears.

"Push her."

I wondered if I'd have any last words for my mother when the time finally came. I thought about that last night before I slept. Anything important I should say before the deed is done. This was my chance.

Nothing at all comes to mind.

My hands burst forward with all the force I can muster and hit Filth directly in the chest. My palms send her plummeting down into the hole in the earth. She manages a weak, choked scream as she falls. It makes her sound especially old.

The root cellar is shaking now. Everything is vibrating. I can't see Filth falling because that hole is very dark and seems to stretch down into the realm of forever. I hear a scrabbling sound. Something incredibly large burrowing and ascending through the tunnel-like hole.

I hear a wet splat down in the hole. I hear a muffled old voice screaming my name. There's horror in that voice. It's the sound of someone screaming while in the process of losing their mind, screaming until their very lungs burst inside of them. I hear a terrible crunch. I hear bones cracking like twigs and all the screaming stops.

I hear chewing.

Great, greedy chewing.

A rush of sour wind assaults me and almost knocks me back from the hole. Something gargantuan bursts up out of the darkness like a conqueror worm and spreads many hands outward with many long beckoning fingers. So many eyes see me now. I catch a glimpse of little pieces of my mother caught in teeth the size of jagged tombstones. There are appendages everywhere. There is raw, pulsating flesh everywhere on the thing that is M. I understand immediately that I'm seeing only a little part of him. Only a fragment of the body of M, but it demands to be worshipped.

I only look at M for a second or two but that's all it takes to break whatever is left of my sanity. That's okay. I'm not really all that sad to see it go.

I never was all that sane to begin with.

I kneel before him and cast my eyes to the dirt. My eyes belong on the dirt. No one can gaze too long into the eternal. No eyes are meant for that icy endlessness lest they ooze and drip right out of the sockets.

I fall to my hands and my knees and I kiss the dirt. I let the dust coat my lips. I give all of myself to M. I give him my mind, my body, my soul. A little piece of Filth's shredded face falls down before me and I kiss that too, enjoying the taste of crimson.

A very large hand with very long fingers pats my head. It pats my head like someone would pat the head of a doggie. That's a good girl. That's a very good girl. The fingers stink of death and disease and they make me think of doorways to dark places.

M's touch is revolting and erotic all at the same time.

I like it.

Chapter 43

Thorny Rose

I guess I lost track of time after that. Evening turned to night and all the slivers of light that came through the walls faded into black. M had returned to his pit but still he lingered close, his telekinetic touch occasionally reaching up to brush sweaty hair away from my forehead.

There was an old rusty toolbox down here and I found a claw hammer and some bent nails within it. The claw hammer had a dried maroon stain on the head of it. I wondered about that. I used the hammer to nail the remnants of my mother's face to a support beam near one corner of the root cellar. It was a loose, fleshy mask with torn craters where eyes had once been. It was all that was left of Rebecca Crimshire. The last little piece of Filth remaining in the world.

I wanted it there as a memento.

After it was done I sat cross-legged at the edge of the pit. I twirled my hair in my fingers and rocked back and forth, enjoying the gentle sway of my body so close to the abyss. I listened to the whispers from the deep. Nothing like the whisper in my head. M's voice never wanted me to hurt myself, it only asked me to hurt others. Just hurt the lost ones. The forgotten ones. Those broken, faceless people that move through the world unnoticed. Their lives would be a sacrifice to the appetite of something that has been buried unjustly for far too long. That sacrifice would make M much stronger. It would help him to free himself from his prison in the dirt.

They must die so that M may rise.

He needed blood and flesh and the spirits of the fallen to do that. It was all just fuel for the machine. I'd help him. I'd be his proxy. I'd lure the vagrants here and M would take them. He would feed on them and suck them dry. And then I'd be famous and everyone would love me. I'd finally live up to my true potential.

And most importantly, when my prince Roman wakes from his deep, dark sleep...he will love me most of all. He'll see me as his soul mate. I will be his bright, flickering flame in a world blotted out by M's great shadow.

M showed me so many wonderful visions while I sat with him. He whispered so many lovely promises into my ears. He tickled me beneath my chin and made me giggle and blush.

We made our pact while the torn body of my mother digested in the juices of M's stomachs somewhere far below.

I've got lots of work to do now. Very important work.

Busy little bees are meant to buzz.

That's me.

Just a busy little bee.

Chapter 44

Thorny Rose

I got two of them in that first week. One was so thickly bearded and grimy that I could barely make out the features of his face. He reminded me of a rodent. He stank of cheap booze and unwashed skin. I found him lingering in the food court at Orchard Hill Mall. He had all of his belongings crowded around the table that he sat at in big black trash bags. I knew immediately that he was one of the lost ones. One of the forgotten ones. He would not be missed. His destiny waited behind M's teeth.

I offered him a hot meal and a clean bed. I put just the right inflection of kindness in my voice. He agreed immediately. I was no threat to him, just a cute little goth girl with a generous heart. I never asked his name. The names don't matter to me. His name might as well be dinner.

I drove him back to the root cellar under the cover of a cold, starlit sky. We talked about cats during the drive. He was a big cat person. I'm a pretty big cat person too.

He didn't understand what was happening when I got him close to the hole. It was dark and he was confused. I told him I stored the food down in the hole. The idiot actually leaned down to look. I pulled my straight razor out and in one quick motion I sliced cleanly through his Achilles tendon. That hobbled him immediately. I planted my combat boot on the dusty seat of his jeans and kicked him down into the abyss. He fell for a long time...and then I can only assume he landed in M's mouth. I associated that wet splash with the derelict falling onto one of M's tongues and then strangling in a pool of salty saliva.

Some of that saliva flew up from the pit as M dined on his supper. It was like a very fine rain spraying up from the earth. I stuck out my own tongue and caught a few droplets of it. It tasted a bit like black licorice.

It was all over very quickly.

M always eats them quickly.

The next one was a vulgar little junkie I found shooting up in an alley behind the adult bookstore downtown. He had a lazy eye and he kept calling me "baby." He was very thin, almost emaciated. He'd probably be crunchy...but I didn't think M would mind. I promised him the best heroin of his life with a complimentary blowjob for the grand finale. He followed me back to my car after that like a panting puppy.

It was almost too easy.

I told him I wanted to suck him off in a dark, lonely place. I said I wanted to get kinky. I told him all about the mattress I kept in a shallow hole in my root cellar. I kissed him deeply as I edged him closer to the pit. He tasted like cigarettes and failure. I waited until we were inches from the chasm before I buried my knee into his genitals and pressed my index finger against his forehead.

He was already doubled over and it only took a little tap to send him flying downward to his doom. I leaned over and watched. A big chunk of his headless torso flew halfway up the pit before gravity took hold and brought it crashing back down into the blackness. I applauded M for that one.

What a wonderful show!

M kept getting stronger. He kept getting hungrier too. Some nights he wanted me to dig around the hole. He told me the hole has to be much, much bigger. It was hard work for a little thing like me but I swung that pick with lots of gusto and even whistled while I worked.

The hole kept getting bigger. It was the size of almost three big graves all connected together now. The ragged, rotting face of Filth watched me from the support beam as I worked.

I'd have to keep hunting. I'd have to keep digging too.

I guess this kind of work isn't really for everyone. I'm good at it, though. I don't have any empathy for the lost and forgotten ones. They're homeless and stinky and I like the sounds their bodies make when they're being shredded into tiny pieces.

Gotta keep digging and hunting until M is able to crawl up out of his hole.

I'm gonna hug him so tight when he finally does!

Chapter 45

Thorny Rose

I've stopped going to my job at the library. They called and left voicemails but I just ignored them. Life had given me a big promotion and I just didn't have the time to work two jobs right now. Sometimes you reach a fork in the road and have to decide where you want the future to take you. This was my crossroads.

I chose M. I chose digging and hunting. I had responsibilities. It was my job to make sure the meat was tenderized before it went down into the hole. This girl is all about chasing her dreams. I started singing in the shower. My voice has always been scratchy and off-key, pretty much incapable of putting together any sound that resembles a pleasant melody. Not anymore. I have the voice of a rock goddess now. I can belt out haunting ballads and make the shower curtain tremble with the ululations that fall from my lips. I sound like one of the Greek sirens capable of luring sailors to a watery doom.

M kept giving me these little gifts along the way. I was being groomed for the world stage. I was evolving, becoming something so much greater than the weak, frail little creature that I used to be. One morning I woke up in bed and looked at myself in the mirror, already reaching for my glasses. It took me a moment to realize that my vision was crystal clear now and I didn't even need them anymore. My gray eyes were like chips of stone staring back at me and they showed me everything in high definition. M later told me that he needed my eyes to be keen so that it would be easier for me to track down the lost ones.

I threw my glasses into the garbage disposal and never looked back.

After hunting I'd come home to my quiet, empty house and I'd enjoy the peaceful confines of the hoard maze. It wasn't so bad anymore now that Filth had been dethroned, the rat queen dead and digested. I'd inherited her kingdom.

M gave me bright, shiny stones from the earth and I'd pawn them for money. Diamonds and sapphires and jewels pulled from the layers of soil below my feet. I bought and ate whatever food I wanted. I brought home whole sacks filled with books. I added entirely new serial killer posters to my collection.

This huge glossy poster of Richard Ramirez now graces the ceiling just above my bed. I get to fall asleep each night with the Night Stalker looking down at me.

Talk about hot. Those cheekbones...

I even bought a book about this local Rust Valley legend from way back in the 1960s. Nothing was ever confirmed because no bodies were ever found, but James Silver was rumored to have killed numerous prostitutes around town back in those old days. He was a carpenter and the newspapers labeled him Gentleman James because he used to wear these really sharp suede suits. One night he parked his truck on Flaggwood Bridge and blew his own head off with a sawed-off shotgun. The police found little fragments of his skull washed up on the banks of the Potomac River.

After his suicide they searched his cabin in the woods outside of Rust Valley. They found burnt bundles of women's clothing in the wood stove. The articles of clothing belonged to the prostitutes that turned up missing during that scorching hot summer in the swinging sixties. One of the hottest summers in Rust Valley's recorded history.

Gentleman James left a suicide note but the book doesn't have many details about what he wrote. That sucks. The whole story is really interesting.

I feel like I'm transforming just like the serial killers I idolize transformed before me. I'm becoming a member of a very exclusive club. Each time I hunt down a lost one and take them to the pit, I'm crossing further and further into the land of taboo. Their ends make M stronger, and in turn, M makes me stronger.

I love my own reflection now. I've tossed away all my bulky old sweaters. I wear tight black tank tops now and have taken to tying my hair up into bouncy pigtails. My body is changing too. My breasts are fuller, my hips rounder, my waist smaller. I'm attaining a perfect hourglass shape. My new favorite checkered skirt barely comes halfway up my thighs and does a great job of showing off the new curves. I decorate my legs in black fishnets and holy fuck, my legs are *killer*.

I don't cover my scars anymore. I keep my arms bare, the scars like beautiful discolored snakes traveling all the way up the length of my arms. I'm tired of hiding.

I have only one tattoo. I got it when I turned eighteen as my first act of rebellion and kept it a secret from Filth ever since. It's a skull right in the middle of my chest between my breasts, the outline etched into my skin with stark black ink.

I've made a new addition to my tattoo.

I carved the letter M directly into the center of the skull with my straight razor. The wound bled and then dried up, becoming the perfect dark scab to match the tattoo ink surrounding it. I'm looking at my new artwork in my room's shattered mirror.

I feel incredibly attractive.

I need to look my best for Ro when he finally wakes up.

My Ro.

Chapter 46

Thorny Rose

I curled up like a kitten that night, my fluffy comforter pulled close and my feet hanging off the edge of the bed. I'd just painted my toenails and I was admiring the glossy black of the polish as I started to doze off into sleepytown. My newly purchased stereo system plays in the background, Motionless In White serenading me with beautifully dark melodies as I drift slowly away.

I was very tired and I'd hoped for dreamless sleep. That didn't happen. I felt the real world fade away and immediately another world replaced it. I rarely ever dream so I was a bit surprised when I opened my eyes to a surreal environment that stood out in incredibly vivid detail. I knew instantly that I was dreaming. Everything about my surroundings was just slightly off. The moon was enormous in the sky and I could count every crater on the surface. The stars were brighter than ever, like giant headlamps set into a circular sky. I hated the shine of them.

I didn't like it here at all.

I was standing on a vast tundra, a desert of ice stretching around me on every visible horizon. The wind cut through me like a refrigerated blade and threatened to pick me up and take me away. Heavy snowfall fell from above, covering everything. The mountains in the distance were snowcapped and icy. The strange thing about them was that they looked almost slightly familiar, like the same range of mountains that cuts around Rust Valley. This couldn't be the town I grew up in though. This was a frozen world decorated in ice crystals and every breath I took into my lungs seemed to burn.

I knew if this wasn't just a dream I'd probably be dead of frostbite within minutes. I was wearing nothing but my tank top and Batman undies. Not really the best choice for arctic weather. My bare feet were lost in the snow, covered up to the knees. Big and furry animals lumbered across the snow near the edge of the mountain range. They looked like woolly mammoths.

I spun around and stumbled, trying to shield my eyes against the glare of the whiteout. Someone was walking towards me through the snowfall. One second he was very far away, a pinprick in the distance...and the next he was standing barely a few feet in front of me.

It wasn't a man. It was a revenant who used to be a man. It stood there before me, staring with a jaw barely hanging together by a few stringy pieces of muscle and sinew. The tattered corpse wore a dirty brown suit that was defiled by grave soil. Something about his eyes unsettled me. As the snowfall calmed down a bit I noticed that he didn't have eyes at all, just balls of wriggling tubifex worms in the empty sockets where his eyes used to be.

I didn't know what he wanted. It seemed suddenly like the corpse and I were in some kind of force field, the blizzard blazing outside of it but everything calm and quiet within. He turned to point one desiccated finger towards the surface of an iceberg chunk jutting up out of the snow. I had time to notice an old gaping wound on the back of his head, all cratered meat and mummified blood. It looked like the result of shrapnel from a very powerful firearm passing through his skull.

I heard a wretched screeching sound as he pointed towards the iceberg and it took me a moment to realize that a message was being scraped into the ice while I watched. It happened extremely fast, the words forming within seconds.

"*Do not be his puppet.*"

"*Do not let him use you and throw you away.*"

"*Do not lose yourself to his will and his wants.*"

"*He corrupts and he deceives and he will kill everything that you are, everything you used to be.*"

I stared at the message. My eyes glimmered beneath the bright stars and the gargantuan moon. Everything I used to be? I used to be weak. I used to be pathetic. I used to be shunned. The dead man is twirling his finger again, the ice chips flying as new words carve through the surface.

"This is Rust Valley."

"Another time, another era. Long ago."

"He wants to devour the world."

"He must remain below."

The corpse in the dirty brown suit gestures downward in a sweeping motion and all the snow gets literally pushed away on all sides of us, mountainous amounts of snow moving away from us and uncovering the surface that we're standing on.

It's vast and milky. You can just see through it. It's the icy surface of a huge frozen lake. There is something beneath the ice that is equally huge. Almost as big as the lake itself. It is perfectly still and unmoving down there, trapped within the ice. It's extremely hard to see details through the ice but I can tell that it's some sort of body down in the lake. Some *thing* with thousands of limbs and the kind of incomprehensible anatomy that makes my mind feel like it's twisting in on itself.

Suddenly I'm very tired of this. I don't want to be in this dream with this stupid corpse anymore. This is my head the revenant is infiltrating. It's my head, my world, my dream. All mine to mold.

I start to concentrate very hard on the dreamscape around me. I bring my hands up in front of me and mime what I want the world to do, twisting them and squeezing them together. The reality of the dream contorts. The snow flies away. The ice melts. The lake vanishes underfoot right along with the thing that dwells below.

The corpse in the dirty brown suit looks around, perplexed as he takes in his new surroundings. He's in a vast great room lit by many blazing torches. My old tormentors from school howl all around the big room, all of them trapped in unforgiving torture devices. Some of them claw and reach through gibbets. Some hang nailed to the walls, crucified and disemboweled. Others hang from the ceiling from nooses, twirling and blue-faced. The centerpiece of the room is a rectangular pool of noxious green acid. Most of the former bullies swim and suffer in this pool, their flesh slowly sloughing off as their bodies become nothing but red and ruined gloop.

I sit on a throne built of picked bones, some animal, some human. I wear a flowing black latex gown with a vulture skull broach between my cleavage. My long black hair moves through the air, reaching and questing like tentacle strands. There is sprawling scarlet drapery behind me that never seems to end.

I gaze down at the corpse from my throne, a smile pulling back my lips. My teeth are all filed down to points and my tongue is forked through the middle. I speak to him with thunder; I punctuate my point with lightning.

"He will rise."

The corpse in the dirty brown suit hangs his head. His expression conveys defeat and disappointment. Even through the thin and mummified flesh, I can read the look on his face.

He sees me as a lost cause.

He turns and walks away, leaving dirty footprints on the floor of my great room. He brings his finger up and twirls it as he goes, wispy white words forming in the very air before my throne.

"You are too far gone."

I seethe. I hate him. I want to rip his dead body open and eat his decomposed heart. His words are shit. He is nothing, he is dead and forgotten and I want to bring him back to life just so that I can kill him all over again.

I scream and I scream and the eardrums of all of my tormentors burst simultaneously.

I awaken.

Chapter 47

Thorny Rose

I guess that dream was meant to dissuade me. That stupid, worthless dead man was trying to turn me away from my chosen path. He failed. If anything he sent me blazing in the opposite direction. I'm more motivated than ever before now and I'll scrape at the pit with my bare hands until my fingernails crack and bleed and snap off if that's what it takes to free M from the bowels of the earth.

I got another three this week. I barely even remember their faces. Just grimy homeless scumbags pulled up from the gutters of society and thrown down into the hole. M chewed them all up and belched out a few bits of their broken bones.

They followed me back to the root cellar like lost lambs eager to be herded by a shepherd. I delivered them to the dirt king and now they suffer forever in his castle of everlasting soil. I'm a good little hunter. M tells me that often. He praises me. Filth never praised me. She never appreciated me or respected me.

Fuck her. I hope she's being split wide open by devil cock in the deepest, hottest part of Hell. I'm destined for big things. There is nothing and no one that can stop me now. If the cops ever sniff me out and find out what I've done I'll cut them and kill them and cast them down into the darkness where many rows of teeth will be waiting for them.

My count stands at six...but I want more. I hunt and I search and I locate the perfect seventh. I find him sitting in the back of a local soup kitchen and slurping charity noodles through his lips and down into his blubbery stomach. He is a huge, bulbous man, easily weighing in at three hundred pounds. His hair is long and greasy and there are disgusting lesions that decorate his face.

I sit with him and I weave my lies, each one more promising than the last. I tell him there's a fully stocked bomb shelter beneath my house and he can stay there for as long as he likes. He'll have a roof over his head and all the surplus food he can possibly eat. His little piggy eyes brighten immediately, a wet tongue slipping out to lick sore-covered lips. He gobbles up the remainder of his noodles and then tilts the bowl back to let the broth rain down his throat. He wipes a meaty forearm across his mouth and lifts one glazed ham of an ass cheek and honks out the loudest fart I've ever heard in my lifetime.

That's all the signal I need. We leave together after that, the little goth girl and the corpulent hog lumbering along beside her. Such an odd couple. We could star in our own sitcom if I wasn't planning on feeding the fat man to something with an appetite far greater than his own.

There was one worrying moment when I thought the fat man wouldn't fit through the root cellar's door, but he worked hard to push his girth through the threshold, his flab dragging up against crumbling plaster siding. He goggled around the room while picking at his sores.

"Where's the food?" His voice is nasally, choked with phlegm and half-digested chicken noodle soup.

He's totally ignorant of the fact that he's standing with his back inches away from the edge of the pit. I step towards him softly while pulling my straight razor from my back pocket. I'm very close to him now, smiling up into his pockmarked moon of a face. He dwarfs me in both weight and height.

"You're the food."

I swing my left fist up into an arching uppercut that catches the shelf of the fat man's jaw. Under normal circumstances his blubber would probably absorb the blow and I'd likely break my hand. These are not normal circumstances. The uppercut shatters the fat man's jaw instantly. The crack of it is like a pistol going off in the cramped confines of the root cellar.

I'm pretty fucking strong now. M spoils me with these little gifts. I have the reflexes of a jungle cat and the strength to smash a human skull into bone dust.

I feel thick sausage fingers close around my throat and a muddled "Bishtchhh" exits the broken mush of the fat man's mouth. This game just keeps getting more exciting. He's good sport!

His shit-brown eyes widen in shock when I flick the straight razor out from behind my back. I bury it deeply into the meat of his abdomen and I twist oh so sweetly back and forth. Blood bubbles pop in his nostrils and his grip on my neck weakens. I withdraw the razor, the blade slick with plasma and little chunks of his internal organs. Next I reach into the wound with my bare hand and dig around like a little girl searching for a treat...and oh goodness, I find one!

My hand closes around a slithery rope of intestine and I yank it out in one good pull, little dribbles of fecal matter and bile splashing out across my wrist. The malodorous giant moans and stumbles backward. I let him fall...but I don't release the length of intestine. He plummets like a deflating zeppelin and his guts unfurl out of him with each twist and turn he makes now that he's picking up speed. His rotund mass slams up against the earthen walls of the hole and finally his girth becomes *lodged* somewhere down in the pit.

He brays at me like a mutilated mule. I can just barely see the sweat glistening on his shiny moon face somewhere down in the darkness. I can't help but chuckle, the long rope of intestine trailing down into the pit like a red and dripping life preserver. Finally I just toss the length of guts down there with the rest of him. I flick the slime from my palm and wipe it off on the back of my pants.

I've never seen one of the lost ones actually get stuck in the hole before. I have absolutely no idea what happens next. My answer comes in the form of an impossibly long and spindly arm that bursts up through the fat man's unseen anus and out of his screaming mouth, the long pale fingers closing around the face and body of the prey before dragging it down into the blackness beyond the scope of my vision. Little pieces of the fat man's body glisten on the tunnel walls after he gets pulled down into oblivion.

M takes his time with this particular meal. It's one of the biggest he's had in a long time. I assume he starts with the legs because I can still hear the weak and dying screams from somewhere below. They are symphonies of suffering.

My count stands at seven now. I can't help but feel proud of myself.

I'm doing this for me and my Ro.

I'm doing this for *us.*

He'll understand when he wakes up.

Part III:
Dirty Secrets

Chapter 48

Roman

I've been floating in a dark sea for what seems like a long time now. It's warm and inky and it's not really such a bad place. I'm comforted by the constant nothingness and the weight of the silence that blankets me. I understand on some deep, instinctual level that I've been hurt very badly and I'm trapped in the empty depths that lie between life and death. I'm not cut off from the world of the living completely. Occasionally I'll hear snippets of conversation drift down to me from somewhere far away and far above.

My mother's voice. My father's voice. The voices of unfamiliar nurses and doctors. I've been able to glean that my parents aren't staying at the house in Rust Valley right now. They've temporarily moved in with my aunt in Baltimore, Maryland. She lives near the Inner Harbor. They're staying with her so that they can be closer to me. I picked up enough little bits and pieces of distant conversation to know that my broken body has been transported to Mercy Medical Center in Baltimore.

I'm very happy about the fact that my folks aren't staying at the house in Rust Valley. I want them to be very far away from that house and outside of the town limits. I'm not exactly sure why, my memories seem fragmented now and it's hard to put the jigsaw pieces together. All I know for certain is that there's something very bad beneath Rust Valley. Something that infects the very ground of the town and makes my haunted head flash with images of centipedes and blood running down into fissures in the dirt.

I don't know how long I've been down here in the dark. Time has no meaning in a place like this. I just swim through the endless emptiness and I never break the surface. I'm not even sure that there is a surface to break.

I keep trying, though. There's the nagging thought that I have unfinished work to do beyond the blackness. Something incredibly important. Something pivotal that is calling me back from death's final door. I can't remember what it is. I can't remember much of anything now.

I think I see something out there in the void that surrounds me. That cannot be. This is a nothing place. There cannot be something in a nothing place. But there is something. There's a figure floating towards me through space and time and the umbilical cord that connects the living to the dead. I've seen him before. He holds a special place somewhere in the fragmented remnants of my memory.

He floats close to me and then he stops. He left a trail of dust through the nothingness behind him. His suit is very dirty and befouled, the material seeming to rot right off of his gaunt form. He is a dead thing, all dried up with worms where his eyes should be. He opens his mouth to speak but he cannot speak. There's a big hole in the back of his head and I can see right through it. His tongue is nonexistent, vaporized by whatever trauma put the hole in his head and killed him.

He is reaching for me. His hands are bony and his fingernails have grown long and sharp due to his long stint in the grave. He grips my cheeks gently with those mummified hands and immediately the memories flood in. I was empty and broken but I'm being filled up again, I'm being fixed. He gives me back what I lost.

I remember everything.

I remember the crash, I remember the root cellar...and I remember the hungry fiend that lives below. I remember threats and lies and a single letter that brings fresh fury into my resurrected heart.

M.

The corpse in the dirty brown suit is very close now, inches away from my face. I can see that his skin is peeling off from the bone like chipped paint from an abandoned house. His lips move but no words come out. Even though I cannot hear his message to me, I'm able to see the worms squirming down from his eye sockets to take up residence on his frail and sunken chest. The worms are linking together and spelling out letters, forming words.

I gaze down at the message the corpse has crafted for me. Just three slimy worm-words that leave me deeply curious.

"See through me."

I'm not sure what any of this means but I get the sense that the corpse wants my permission to do something. I nod my affirmation to him. The dead thing draws me closer and presses his forehead against my own. I gaze into the hollow sockets where his eyes used to be. I gaze long and I gaze deep.

I see through him...

Chapter 49

Gentleman James (Dreamscape)

It was the summer of 1968 in Rust Valley, West Virginia. The sun was like a furnace hanging low in the sky and sending out heat waves the likes of which the town had never seen before. You could barely walk a few steps down Main Street without sweat dripping down your brow and stains forming beneath your armpits. It was hellish, muggy weather...and for me it was a hellish, muggy year.

I'd lost my little daughter Maggie earlier that spring. She was only seven, the apple of my eye. She was swinging high and enjoying the smell of honeysuckles in the air when she fell off the swing and just laid there still. My wife and I ran across the playground and grabbed her up and loaded her in the back of my Dodge Charger and tore down to the hospital as fast as we possibly could.

She was already dead and cold by the time we got her through the doors. The doctors told us it was a brain aneurysm, very sudden and totally unpredictable.

It devastated us. She was our only child. They buried her in a little open coffin in her prettiest sundress with a bouquet of yellow daffodils in her tiny cold hands. Maggie always loved daffodils. I remember shaking hands at that funeral and being looked at with such stark pity in the eyes of my friends and my family. They looked at me like I was a dog run down on the highway, a dog that didn't know how badly he was torn up yet.

I felt like I'd been gutted. Some essential part of me had been removed by the loss of Maggie and I knew in my heart nothing would ever fill that hole up again. I tried to make it work with Carol. I tried to be the rock that she needed. She became distant and morose. Our marriage became loveless and the arguments reigned. Maggie was the sweet yellow daffodil that brightened our lives and now that it had been uprooted there wasn't much brightness left for us.

We divorced a few months after her death. Carol moved back to her hometown in Boston and I remained there in Rust Valley. I worked as a carpenter in those days. I made good money. The locals knew me because I'd always come to their door wearing a crisp brown suit of the finest suede with my toolbox in hand and my midnight black Dodge Charger idling in the driveway.

I poured myself into my work after my daughter died and my wife left me. I labored long hours and focused purely on the task at hand. I didn't want to think about that hole in my heart. If I hammered the nails in loud enough it would drive my grief away, if only for a little while. I'd taken to drinking in my spare time. I'd drown my thoughts with whiskey and I'd lie there in my empty cabin and think about taking a length of rope and putting an end to things. I'd think about going to see my Maggie.

I don't even remember how the job came to me. It was just one of those contracts that came down the pipeline and landed in front of me. It was a ramshackle house on Legion Lane that had been rebuilt and halfway remodeled time and time again. It was an ugly ol' mutt of a place and I didn't hold out much hope for it the first time I saw it. The company I worked under just wanted me to take stock of what needed fixing and do what I could before the owners put it up for rent again.

I did a walkthrough in early June. Couple faucets needed replacing in the kitchen. The roof needed to be shingled and patched in a few spots. One of the bedroom doors was hanging off the hinges and that would need to be dealt with too. There wasn't anything all that remarkable about the interior of the place. Looked about like any other old house I'd seen on the job. I made some notations in my little notebook and moved on to get a look at the outside.

The foundation of the place seemed decent enough. The yard was overgrown and the grass desperately in need of some mowing. There was only one section of the property that seemed a bit odd to me. It was a swampy patch of land near the back of the house, the whole area shrouded in low hanging willow trees and gnarled thorn bushes. I didn't think there was much of anything back there but I checked it out anyway.

I came across a little door that lead down into the earth. I hadn't been told about any basement so I assumed this was a root cellar. The door was made up of old, rotten wood and a few lazy green flies buzzed around the entrance. I opened her up and pushed my way inside.

There wasn't much to be seen in the dark little confines. Couple ragged support beams and walls that had seen much better days. The floor was hard-packed dirt and there was a powerful stink down here that I couldn't place. Smelled kinda like something sweet that had gone ripe and sour. I took a few more notes and was about to head out when my daughter's voice called up to me.

"Daddy?"

I dropped my toolbox and it landed with a clatter. I must have imagined that.

It came again, just as sweet and innocent. There was no mistaking my Maggie's voice.

"Is it you up there, Daddy?"

I was feeling terribly confused. Beads of sweat were popping out on my brow and my heart couldn't seem to settle into a normal pace. I looked down at the dirt to try and find an explanation for this. All I saw was a tiny hole there at my feet, circular and about the size of a penny. The slightest draft of cold, dank air wafted up from the little hole. My daughter's voice followed the draft.

"Please talk to me, Daddy. I'm so alone down here. It's dark and cold and there ain't no sun for the daffodils."

Tears were cutting down through the lines of my face. None of this made any damn sense, but I couldn't deny the longing in her voice. She needed her father. She was hurting and she was cold and she needed Daddy to protect her just like I'd always done for her.

"Maggie...is that you, baby girl? Is that really you?"

I crouched down by that tiny hole and I stay crouched down for a long time. Maggie's voice echoed up to me from somewhere deep underground. She told me she was dead and locked away in a forgotten place. She said God couldn't take her up to heaven because her little soul got stuck down in the dirt. She told me it hurts so much to be dead. She told me she was so hungry. She told me she was starving.

I cried and I listened, my tears dripping down into the little hole as she spoke to me. She told me she was suffering and the pain was unbearable. She asked me to help her. My Maggie told me that there was a way for her to come back to the land of the living again. She said I'd have to bring her people to eat. She said the only way for the dead to rise is if they eat the flesh and the spirits of the living.

She said I'd need to kill for her if I wanted us to be a family again. I'd never killed a person in my whole life. The whole idea seemed insane...but I wasn't thinking clearly. My heart was hammering and seemed fit to burst with love for my little dead daughter. She was my whole world and I wanted her to come back to me more than anything else in life.

I told her I'd need to think about this. I told her I'm not a killer and I don't think I can do this. It broke my heart even more to tell her these things when she was down there in the earth hurting and begging me to bring her back to life again.

Something happened that made my mind up for me. She pushed a few bright yellow daffodils up through the tiny hole. I never saw her little hand and I don't know how she reached up that far...but somehow she did. I brought them up to my nose and I inhaled deeply. The scent of my only daughter. The little blonde beauty that I'd move mountains for.

Her voice followed the flowers.

"Please, Daddy..."

I kept on smelling the flowers. I kept on thinking about my daughter's face.

"I love you."

My fist tightened around the stems. My resolve hardened. My tears dried up and my decision was made. I would need to be strong for Maggie. I would need to make sacrifices and do dirty, awful work to resurrect my little girl.

That was the moment James Silver died.

That was the moment Gentleman James was born.

Chapter 50

Gentleman James (Dreamscape)

I started cruising through the bad parts of town late at night. The working girls would get a look at me, a man with a nice car and a ruggedly handsome face, and they'd push their breasts out as far as they could and wave at me as I passed. I'd never picked up a prostitute before. I didn't even know what the hell I was doing until I finally pulled over and the first girl came up to my open window. She had bottle blonde hair with dark roots starting to show through and her lips were glazed with candy apple gloss. It didn't take much talking to get her in the passenger seat. She had a deep country twang in her voice and she whispered all the dirty things she was gonna do to me in my ear as I drove down dark and wooded roads.

I told her to close her eyes and wait for the surprise as I lead her into the root cellar. She was giggly and expectant, wouldn't stop running her hands across my chest. She didn't even seem to notice when her high heels sank down into the soil. I didn't want her to look at me so I spun her gently around and had her face the wall, her hands still clamped playfully over her eyes.

I swallowed and fought deeply against my conscience. It kept telling me not to do this. Kept saying it's not too late to turn back. The memory of Maggie picking daffodils in a beautiful wild field is what finally made me swing the claw hammer and bash the whore's brains out. She fell with a hollow plop sound, not totally dead but broken beyond all repair. I felt sick to my stomach after doing it. She was convulsing there on the dirt floor when something hideous happened to her.

Her flesh got sucked down into that tiny little hole. That's the only way I can describe it. I guess Maggie managed to snag a little piece of her skin and just yank and pull the whore downward. Her skin was stripped off like tape and it vanished into the dirt right along with her muscle tissue and everything else. All that remained was a steaming wet skeleton.

The sight made me feel like I'd been riding a rollercoaster all day, my stomach leaping up and down and tying itself into knots. Maggie thanked me afterwards. She said it made her feel a little better. She told me it took away some of the pain of being dead.

It was only the beginning. I repeated this act with four more prostitutes. Over the course of that summer I picked them up and drove them back to the root cellar and hit them with the hammer and fed them all to my little dead daughter. At one point she asked me to take a pick to the hole and make it a little bigger so she could eat the bones too. I did that for her. I'd do just about anything for her.

I asked all the whores to strip down first and then I'd burn their clothes in the wood stove back at my cabin. I started to hate myself for what I was doing. I knew it was wrong. I knew I was being selfish and evil and I was ending lives but I loved my daughter immensely and I understood the price going into this.

The more she ate, the more a lingering doubt was eating at me. My daughter was a kind, innocent creature in life. She loved animals and she hated the idea of harming anything. I tested her one night while gathering up clothes after she had just fed. I asked her what color dress she wanted me to buy her when she's alive and well again. She told me purple, her favorite color.

Purple was not Maggie's favorite color. It was yellow. That fueled into my doubt even more. She told me for the next meal, I would need to get something special for her. She told me to volunteer my time as a substitute bus driver at South Woods Elementary School and then drive the busload of children back to the hole. She wanted me to feed her children. She promised that would make her all better and she'd rise up and be herself again after that.

I did as I was asked. I got the gig as a substitute bus driver with South Woods and one evening I drove the busload of kids down Legion Lane, all of them chattering and excited to be going home. I caught a glimpse of my own eyes in the rear view mirror. They were haunted with dark hollows beneath them.

I stopped the bus halfway down Legion Lane. I looked back at the kids, so many young, innocent lives. Young and innocent...just like Maggie used to be. My little daughter would never ask me to do this. My Maggie's favorite color was yellow, not purple. Everything was wrong. I understood that I'd been lead astray.

I called the school and told them the bus had broken down, asked them to send another bus to get the kids. I left the bus and took my satchel with me. I had a sawed-off shotgun in the satchel. Maggie thought it would be best if I used it on the kids before I sent the meat down to her.

I walked aimlessly into someone's yard and opened up the door of their rusty Ford truck. I found the keys still in the ignition. I got behind the wheel and I drove the old truck down to Flaggwood Bridge and parked it there. Flaggwood Bridge never got much traffic and I just sat there for most of the evening and watched the sun set in a beautiful blue sky. I spent most of that evening thinking and writing in my notepad.

As the last rays of sunshine vanished over the mountains I put the sawed-off shotgun into my mouth and I pulled the trigger. The shrapnel tore all my thoughts away and forged my place as a Rust Valley legend for all the years to come. The last sound I heard before the blackness took me was my own blood pattering down against the note on my chest.

"I have done terrible things. I am sorry for all of it. My sins can never be washed away and I've earned my place in Hell. The guilt I feel down there will burn me deeper than the flames ever will.

I thought I was doing this for my daughter. I thought I was helping her. I was deceived. I do not know what lives beneath that house on Legion Lane. I know only that it is malevolent and insatiable and it will never stop until it gets what it wants. It has used me as a marionette and now I've been forced to cut the strings.

It is not my daughter.

It is not my Maggie."

- James Silver, 1968

They buried me in my best suede suit.

Chapter 51

Roman

I see it all through the eyes of Gentleman James. I see how M manipulated him and subsequently destroyed him. I see the last few months of his life in darkly vibrant detail. I can practically feel it when the shotgun blasts goes off in his mouth and kills him. I die with him. I feel what he feels in his grave. I feel his thirst for vengeance.

When the images stop flashing I float a few feet away and see James in an entirely new light. I'm no longer staring at a corpse in a dirty brown suit. I see a handsome man with slick black hair combed back from his forehead. His sharp suede suit looks impeccably clean. I actually hear him when he speaks to me, his tongue whole in his mouth.

"You have to go back, Roman. You're the only one that can finish this."

I want to go back. I want to punish M for all the ugly things he's done.

"I know what M is, Roman. The moment I died the truth of M was revealed to me. He is the voracious one, the eater of all things that live and breathe. M the Unknowable, M the Old Glutton King in the Dirt."

I float and I listen. James's eyes are very blue and very wise.

"He has your friend in his thrall now. She cannot be saved. M compels, as he did with you and I. But Rose is not just compelled. Rose is doing M's work because she likes it. She is the perfect proxy...and even now they plot to bring the heavy machinery to Legion Lane. M is tired of his prison. M wants to be dug out. He wants to rise."

Rose is involved in this? That fucking MONSTER has his claws in her too?

"If they start digging with the heavy machines it will never stop until they break through the walls of M's prison. That's the end for everyone, Roman. That will mark the extinction of

the human race. There's still time to stop them...but you have to hurry."

James is reaching towards me, his hands splaying out to grab the sides of my head as he once again presses his forehead up against my own.

"I'll help you as much as I can. Take my strength. Take my energy. Take my vengeance."

The dark sea is flickering all around us. I see flashes of fluorescent lights and beeping medical equipment.

"Take through me."

"Awake through me."

James uses all of his force to fling me upwards at a phenomenal speed, almost like he's giving me a boost. The dark sea flies back on all sides and I finally see the surface in the distance.

I'm about to break through it.

Chapter 52

Roman

My eyes snap open. I tear breath back into dormant lungs. Everything is sore. My whole body feels like it's filled with pins and needles. There's a cast on my left wrist and my ribs are heavily taped up. My right leg is suspended and splinted. Most of the visible flesh on my arms is tattooed with deep purple bruising. I understand immediately that my injuries were much worse but something Gentleman James sacrificed has given me a real chance here.

I'm beaten and battered, but I'm still whole. I'm not a comatose husk languishing in bed while M plots his escape. I wiggle the toes of my right foot and realize that I should be able to walk. I pull the IV out of my forearm in one quick motion, a little droplet of blood appearing along the crease of my elbow. I gingerly sit up in the hospital bed and start to brush the electrodes off my chest.

I bring my bare feet down to the floor and test them. I haven't been comatose long enough for my limbs to atrophy and they manage to support my weight. I lean heavily against the wall and catch a glimpse of myself in a mirror near my bedside. My face is pale, ashen...and I've lost quite a bit of weight. I'm still alive though. That's all that matters.

Night has fallen outside; I can see the starlit sky through my window. Judging by the height of my hospital room I estimate that I'm probably on the sixth floor. Already I'm shrugging out of the thin hospital gown and grabbing my clothes from the little room's closet. I pull on my mud-stained jeans and buckle my boots. I push my arms through the wrinkly t-shirt and wrap my overcoat around my shoulders.

Thankfully my folks are nowhere in sight. I assume they've gone back to my aunt's house for the night. I poke my head out the door and see exactly what I want to see, a deserted hallway. I stumble and stagger my way to the elevator and stab the button until the doors slide open.

I ride it down to the bottom floor. I have one tense moment where I have to hide behind a laundry bin while waiting for two nurses to pass around the corner. Once they're out of sight I dart towards the blinking red of the emergency exit at the end of the corridor and I emerge out into the cold, foggy night.

I have absolutely no plan for transportation back to Rust Valley.

I realize now that I won't need a plan. There's a midnight black 1968 Dodge Charger idling right outside the door. The key is in the ignition and the engine is a beast beneath the hood just waiting to roar. I open the driver's side door and I slide behind the wheel, my foot smashing down on the gas pedal as I burn rubber out of that parking lot.

I catch the turnpike to I-70 and I start heading west in the direction of Rust Valley. The radio automatically clicks into life and "Don't Fear The Reaper" by Blue Oyster Cult pounds out of the speakers to compete with the sound of the engine. I push down harder on the gas pedal and I drive the dead man's car as fast as she'll go.

My headlights cut into the fog as the speedometer passes beyond 80mph.

I push down harder on the gas pedal.

I let the beast roar.

Chapter 53

Thorny Rose

Big things are happening now. There's a darkening on the horizon. There's inevitability in the atmosphere. M is stronger than ever now. He shifts constantly underground and the whole root cellar shakes and trembles. Deep, ragged fissures have opened up around the pit and they snake all across the soil. M is scraping and clawing down in the deep. He's doing his part. He's closer to the surface than he's ever been before. Soon he'll be able to lift *all* of himself out of the pit, not just a little fragment of himself.

I'm doing my part too. I called Greystone Construction and contracted them to start digging a deep quarry here where the root cellar now stands. They'll knock down the walls and use the heavy machines to dig down into the dirt and get to M. They brought the machines out here already. Bulldozers and excavators and rock trucks all sit outside the root cellar, just waiting for the operators to start the excavation process. The construction crew left the property earlier in a few company cars. They'll be returning in the morning and the digging will commence. They think I own the house and the land it sits on. M compelled them to think that. They'll be paid handsomely too. I have a backpack stored in one corner of the root cellar. It's full of sapphires, rubies, diamonds...so many precious stones from below. The backpack is worth a veritable fortune, the contents equating to millions of dollars.

This is my last night as a hunter. Never again will I track down flesh to feed my dirt king in his castle of everlasting soil. He'll walk the world again very soon. He'll do his own hunting then. I will take my place as a queen, an empress, a goddess that will inherit all the riches and pleasures the human world has to offer. I'll sing with the voice of an angelic choir and I'll fuck with the fury of an entire pride of lionesses.

I'll sleep here tonight. I want to be close to the hole. I want to be close to M when he comes so that I can be the first to praise his name. I curl up into the fetal position in the soil and I hold a little ball of Ro's hair in my hands. I ventured into his house earlier today and collected the hair from the comb in his bathroom. It has his smell. His wonderful, delicious aroma carries me down into satisfied sleep.

Soon we'll start our new lives together.

Soon, my Ro.

Soon.

Chapter 54

Roman

I stop at a little gas station in Martinsburg, West Virginia. It's 4am and Rust Valley is just two towns over. Not far now. A light bulb went off in my head and I just had to make a quick stop to get supplies. I purchase a five gallon portable gas can and I fill it to the top with gasoline. I'm standing by the Dodge Charger and pumping the last of the gasoline into the can when I notice a familiar little critter staring at me from the top of the pump.

It's that fucking little house centipede. It waves long antennas at me and twitches at least fifteen pairs of legs together. It almost appears to be dancing.

There's a little piece of yellowing scroll tied to the segmented body with a black silk thread. I don't want to touch this revolting thing because I know it's tied to M somehow, almost like his harbinger of bad omens. I reach forward anyways and pull the thread free to retrieve the note. I unfurl it to see immaculate script written in some sort of red ink. It smells coppery so I assume the ink is blood.

"You never cease to surprise me, child of flesh and sinew! Tough as fucking NAILS, aren't you? Just like your momma! Ha ha! I intended for the car crash to kill you instead of just leaving you comatose. I still considered it a win though because you're not much of a threat to me if you're a brain-dead cucumber down in Baltimore, right?

Imagine my shock when you not only wake up, but jump into this gaudy car and start rolling back to my little neck of the woods. I knew you were spirited...but this is just plain ridiculous. I don't know if it's brain damage or a death wish that spurs you onward, but I suggest you don't cross the town line, Roman. All that's left for you in Rust Valley is pain and ruin between my teeth.

Don't come back here, boy. I will eat you up and shit you out without even breaking stride. I'll rend everything you love until it's nothing but tattered meat and I'll piss on the shallow graves of every single human being on this planet with the unfortunate distinction of having Merrick as a surname.

Long story short: I WILL FUCK YOU UP.

I've met some defiant, overconfidence Homo sapiens in my day but you take the goddamn cake! Stay away. Do not come back here. Turn back now while I'm still willing to place mercy on the table."

- Sincerely, your ol' buddy M

I stand there for a moment, my teeth gritted. The house centipede is still doing that irritating little dance on the top of the gas pump. I ball my fist up and SLAM it down as hard as I possibly can, squashing the house centipede into ruined mush and relishing the satisfying splat sound. I wipe the gunk off on the back of my jeans and slide behind the wheel of the Dodge Charger.

I grin while adjusting the rear view mirror.

Still a few miles to go before I see my "ol' buddy M" again.

Chapter 55

M

I've always been here.

I can't recall if I was born or if I hatched or if one day I just popped into existence. There is no memory of the early years. There was no childhood, no larval stage, no adolescence of any kind. I've been fully grown as far back as I can remember. I recall when most of the world was water and life started to grow down in the deep depths. I'd wade through the oceans and gobble up the new life as soon as it evolved.

I think that was back in the Paleozoic Era. I used to catch these big jawless fish by the dozen and swallow them down without chewing. They were armored and plated so I didn't really like chewing them. They tasted bittersweet.

I enjoyed just letting my body float in the sea back in those old days. Made me feel weightless and free. I'm the largest entity that has ever walked this earth so that sensation was rare for me. I savored it as much as I could.

Time just kept on rolling, a never-ending wheel. I do not age. I do not grow infirm and I never die. Mine is the gift-curse of the eternal. I've never questioned my immortality, I simply accept it.

I'm incapable of seeing my own reflection. I don't know what I look like. I know only what I feel. I know that I have legs like redwoods and more appendages jutting out from my body than I know what to do with. I have eyes all over me and I see from so many different angles. I have many gaping mouths and they're all inlaid with serrated teeth that spin like a circular saw. My digestive tract is the size of a small country and I have stomachs in just about every part of me. Some of them are tumorous and drag across the ground; others are packed together inside me like many stitched together pockets.

The earth quakes when I walk across her surface. My footprints turn into deep ponds when the heavy rain comes. During the Jurassic Era I'd lie back between two volcanoes and I'd wait for the huge sauropods to come tramping through the grasslands below. I'd pinch my long fingers together and way down there in the grasslands the little heads of the dinosaurs would pop like overripe grapes on their long necks. That's how I amused myself back then. I'd laugh and laugh and my laughter always brought the storm clouds.

I've always been telekinetic. I've always been able to compel. I have so many powers and abilities that sometimes I lose track of them all. I get bored with most of them. You would too if you'd been using them for millennia.

My one true drive has always been hunger. I'm always famished and I'm never full. I crave every bit of red, raw flesh that I can bite through. I want all of it inside me. I've devoured species after species, creatures that you won't even find fossil records for because I ate up all the bones and sucked down the marrow.

I had some of my best meals in the Cretaceous Period. Some formidable competition too. That was new for me. I remember those persistent little Velociraptors that would nip at my toes and I'd have to squash whole packs of them. I'd get my real workouts preying on the Tyrannosaurus Rex. They only came up to about chest level, still the size of children to me...but they fought like devils. They'd bite and tear until the last breath. Even took a few good little chunks outta me before I'd inevitably crush them and tear them up into tiny bite-sized pieces.

I have a great respect for those giant lizards. I truly miss the days when dinosaurs populated the earth. I ate my way through them far too quickly and sent almost all of them to the brink of extinction. I should have paced myself a bit more. It saddens me to think that I will never taste their like again.

The last of them died when the flaming asteroid fell from the sky. That left the world scorched for awhile. I laid down for a nap on a field of ash after that. I slept for centuries. I go into a sort of hibernation sometimes and I'm accustomed to waking up in entirely new ages of existence.

I walked the new world for awhile after that. The world turned cold. It became a spinning ball of ice and everything was blanketed in endless snow. It was the most miserable period of my long, strange life. I hated the cold. Mammals rose to prominence and turned this freshly frozen planet into their haven. I'd spend my time wandering the white wastes and chomping down the occasional saber-toothed cat or giant ground sloth. They tasted bland, more fur than meat.

One moonless night I stalked a herd of woolly mammoths as they headed towards a distant mountain range. I planned to take them in the valley below, an endless vista of white that would leave them perfectly vulnerable.

I lumbered towards them, picking up speed. The earth quaked and cracked beneath my feet. I reached out with hundreds of hands all ending in ragged claws to open them up and eat the hot, steaming innards. And then the ground gave way beneath me. I fell through thick layers of ice and down into freezing cold water. I can breathe in water and withstand the deep pressures, but the cold debilitated me. I felt my body temperature dropping and no matter how hard I fought to slither back up to the surface, I continued to sink down lower and lower. My gargantuan weight worked against me. My thoughts grew sluggish and my limbs were growing numb. I felt myself land against the very bottom of the lake.

I had no choice but to enter hibernation. It was my only option. I'd sleep the decades and the centuries away and hopefully when I finally woke up, the water above me would have long thawed and evaporated away.

I closed my thousands of eyes in the murky, frozen depths and slept with my stomachs still gurgling for sustenance.

Chapter 56

M

I wasn't sure how much time had passed when I finally awoke. It felt like thousands of years. I expected to open my many eyes to the sky, either fluffy clouds or bright stars. Instead I opened my eyes to the dim confines of a suffocating prison. The world had grown in around me while I slept. The lower portion of my body was submerged in an underground lake and the upper portion was awkwardly pressed against a cavernous ceiling. I was buried by sediment. Geological formations had formed all around me and if I moved just a few inches in the wrong direction a spiky stalagmite or stalactite would pierce up against my flesh.

Claustrophobia enveloped me. I beat and scraped and clawed at the earthen walls around me but it had no effect. I was weak and withered from starvation. In all of my existence I have never known what it is to be helpless. That changed the moment I realized the dirt had eaten me up. Talk about ironic.

I just languished down in the deep for the first few days. I had almost no room to move around down here. Worms would occasionally wriggle down from above me and I'd catch them on my tongues and greedily suck them down. They did nothing but inflame my hunger even more.

As I stretched my body around I saw one promising opening that cut up through the cavern ceiling. It was rocky and it seemed to lead to upper layers of soil. It was shaped like a small tunnel and if I craned one of my necks around I could just taste a few breaths of fresh air drifting down from at least two miles farther up. I knew that little tunnel opened to the surface. It gave me hope.

One night a small house centipede crawled along the ceiling of my prison. I watched it with thousands of eyes as it explored every crack and crevice. I reached high up and let it crawl onto one of my long fingers. I knew immediately what *needed to be done. I brought the little insectivore to my lips and I gave it a special kiss.*

I imbued it with a fragment of my immortality. I gave it a sliver of my power. It became deathless like me, a creature marked with the gift-curse of the eternal. It became my familiar. It would be my eyes up there. It would show me what the world had become while I slept my frozen sleep.

I sent it back up through the tunnel and it showed me the surface. I saw through the eyes of my familiar. I gasped in the deep. The world was transformed. I saw vast camps and enslaved horses and all manner of unnatural things that had been erected up there. All I remember of mankind is that they were shivering apes that cowered in caves in the age of ice.

Not anymore.

Somewhere along the way, the human race inherited the earth.

My familiar picked up the language of man and brought it back down to me. Every living thing that walks, crawls, or flies in this world has a language. I speak them all eloquently. I have a tongue for every language, each of them collected in one of the chambers of my parasitic mind. It's one of the perks of being the biggest, strongest, smartest thing to ever walk the world.

I learned the hard way that I would not escape this prison without assistance from mankind. I started calling up to them, speaking to them from a voice that echoed through the depths. The Native Americans were the first ones to hear my voice. The Shawnee tribe had a camp not far from my hole. They began to worship me as a spirit of the earth. They formulated a name for me in their language, a guttural word that roughly translated to "Unknowable."

Every month they'd force feed thirteen virgins full of bison meat and then sacrifice them to me by tossing them through the mouth of the tunnel. I'd catch them in midair and grind them up with revolving razor teeth. That was the first time I ever tasted human meat. I had never tasted anything like it. It absolutely intoxicated me. There was something underlying the flesh that lit slow, pleasant fire in my stomachs. The taste fluttered inside of me like a butterfly before growing still. I believe it's the taste of the human soul.

I'd found my perfect delicacy. I needed more. I was absolutely desperate for more. I'd repay the injuns with little gifts. I'd make their crops grow fertile or I'd laugh and make the storm clouds come to bring fresh rain. I was fed and satiated for a few good years. That changed when the white settlers came and brought disease and death to the injuns. I was forgotten.

I slept a lot after that. There wasn't much else to occupy my time. I never slept too long though, just a few decades at a time. I'd learned my lesson about sleeping too long. During my periods of wakefulness I'd spend my time plotting to get out of the hole and scratching at the ceiling of the cavern with the talons that could actually reach up that far. The years passed slowly. Occasionally a human would stumble across the hole and I'd make them my meat puppet for a little while. They'd bring me food and dig from the surface. The sustenance was never enough and the little digging one human could do up there barely ever made a dent in the dirt. Usually these proxies died while in my service. The hole was getting smaller as the earth continued to transform with time. That worried me greatly. I knew if that passageway ever closed, I'd be finished. My familiar would be lost to me and the proxies would have no access to my words. That would lead to endless life and endless darkness and hunger that would drive me mad.

At some point a town was built on the land above me. A house was erected overtop the hole. Civilization marched on.

The hole was painfully small when James came along. I convinced him to open it a little more, and it became a narrow crack. I used the vocal cords of his little daughter to make him feed me. He fed me for awhile and then he stumbled across the truth and put an end to himself. That was frustrating.

I went to sleep after that still frustrated and a few more decades passed. Roman came next. The defiant one. The one

173

that vexed me and questioned me, even managed to use his iron will to shrug off my telekinetic touch. I still can't fathom how he did that...but he will suffer for it.

Thorny Rose followed after. My perfect dark flower. Thanks to her, the hole is not just a hole anymore. It's a pit now, gaping and wide. I can crawl and burrow up just enough to fit a bit of my segmented body into the surface world. She feeds me well. I spoil her because she is my favorite. I feel close to her and perplexed by her all at the same time. She is fiercely loyal but also infinitely strange. Perhaps stranger even than me, in some private, special way.

Others will be coming here soon and they've brought the machines of man with them. They will sink metal buckets into the soil and dig and dig until I'm unearthed. They will drill through the rock and blast away the sediment.

It's about time. I've waited for far too long. I hate it down here. The underground lake that half my body rests in is polluted with my own shit and urine. Infected sores travel along the length of my partially submerged flesh. Maggots often crawl in these festering openings and I can't even reach my hundreds of arms around to scratch at them. I loathe my prison.

I cannot wait to get the fuck outta here...

There are over seven billion human beings alive on the surface right now. That number grows by the second, new mewling infants coming into the world every moment that I'm locked away.

As soon as I'm free...

I think I'll eat them all.

Chapter 57

Roman

I roll into Rust Valley in the hazy predawn hours of what promises to be a gray, cloudy day. It is incredibly cold and the overcast sky looks to be harboring mountains of snow just waiting to fall. The fog is thicker than ever. Visibility is practically nonexistent as I guide the Dodge Charger down Legion Lane.

I drive the roaring hot rod past a few sad and drooping mobile homes before turning down a little twisty curve that leads to the last house in the isolated section of Legion Lane. Wilderness surrounds the house in the distance, the dead trees seeming to stand silent vigil as I approach. I navigate right past the driveway and guide the car through the side yard, letting the tires tear furrows into the dewy ground. I park the car just a few yards away from the entrance to the root cellar. I pop the high beams on, letting the headlights blast through the cracks in the root cellar's walls. I leave the engine on, the powerful V8 not roaring now, but purring in anticipation

I want M to hear me. I want him to know I'm coming for him.

I can see heavy machinery through the fog, the construction equipment standing out like hulking dinosaurs frozen in place. I walk past rock trucks; I circle around a looming bulldozer that rests on gritty tracks. The king of this machine menagerie stands tall just a few feet away from the root cellar's door. It's a Komatsu PC400 excavator. The hydraulic arm snakes downward and the big steel bucket reminds me of a bowing head with ragged teeth. Braham taught me how to operate an excavator years ago when he was still in the construction business. I was counting on this machine being here the moment James mentioned that M was bringing in the heavy artillery. It's the most important part of what comes next. The key to M's downfall.

There's a comforting weight in my right hand. A red can filled to the brim with gasoline, the flammable liquid sloshing around with each step that I take. I stand before that familiar little door. It's a door that might take me to my death. I've accepted that. It's also a door that might lead me towards redemption, and that makes all of this worth the risk. I take my last breath of the cool, frigid air with the morning sun still hiding somewhere low on the horizon. I slam my boot into the door with every bit of strength I have and it explodes inward, the old, rotten wood flying right off the hinges.

There is no fear in me as I stomp through the threshold. Only obligation. Only a sense of responsibility to make my final stand.

I venture into the house of M to I confront the Old Glutton King in the Dirt.

Chapter 58

Roman

The first thing I notice is Rose Crimshire curled up in the corner. The sound of the door crashing inward awakens her and she rubs bleary sleep out of her eyes.

She sees me, *really* sees me, and her gaze widens.

"Ro?"

She turns her attention back to the pit in the center of the root cellar's dirt floor. It's so much bigger than the last time I saw it, gaping open like a slit that leads down to unclean earth. The stench of M is overpowering. It makes my nostrils sting.

"You didn't tell me he was awake, M! This is a wonderful surprise!"

What happens next happens very fast. I sense tremendous rage boiling up out of the pit. The ground shakes so violently that I stumble in place. One of the root cellar's support beams splinters and a whole section of ceiling caves downward.

I feel something like a giant unseen hand slam into my chest and I'm thrown backward against one of the walls, boards flying outward from the impact. The gas can flies out of my hand and lands in the dirt. M bellows from the deep, his voice so loud and warped I feel my very eardrums vibrate at the sound of it.

"YOU STUPID FUCKING MEAT PUPPET...I TOLD YOU TO STAY AWAY!"

I feel long invisible fingers tightening around my throat and pressing me up against the wall of the root cellar. My feet actually leave the floor. I'm choking, my face turning a dark shade of purple. Spittle runs down past my bottom lip.

The world is turning gray.

"NOW YOU DIE...NOW I EAT YOU...NOW I SWALLOW YOUR MINISCULE LIFE, YOU INTERFERING AMOEBA. I'LL SLURP DOWN YOUR GUTS AND I WILL MAKE YOU WATCH."

My vision is fading fast. I can hear a rumbling and scraping from the burrow that snakes down into the deep. M is ascending. M is coming up to feed.

"You're hurting him."

My head cranes weakly around to see Thorny Rose. Her cool gray eyes look incredibly cold and incredibly detached. She is walking towards the pit. She's pulling something from her back pocket. She flicks it open in the darkness of the root cellar. It's shiny and it glimmers. Her expression flickers and contorts.

There's madness and murder in her face.

"You're hurting my Ro."

My head is forced backwards, my airway restricted even more. I can't bear much more of this. Every small thimble of oxygen I get into my lungs becomes a struggle. My entire throat burns with effort. Everything is turning black.

Chapter 59

Thorny Rose

Everything changes the moment M assaults Roman. I don't care about being a queen anymore. I don't care about fame or the adoration of the masses. All those promises wash away in a river of cold hatred and my mind becomes a hornet's nest.

None of it matters now.

The covenant is shattered. M is not my friend anymore. He is a betrayer and a liar and a big bad bully. I hate bullies. Bullies have to bleed. They have to be cut.

My grip tightens on the straight razor in my hand. I stand there above the pit and I gaze down into the darkened depths. M is coming, the whole root cellar shaking violently with the sounds of his ascension.

I guess I'm going to die now.

But before I go...I have a few thorns left specifically for M. There's a lot of ugliness inside of M. I'll cut as much of it out as I can before he gobbles me up.

I dive down into the pit, falling and falling, picking up speed with the straight razor in hand. M ascends, I descend.

Nobody hurts my Ro.

Chapter 60

M

That defiant, ignorant boy. I will choke him until he spits up chunks of his own lungs. He dares to defy the eternal? His life is a mere blink of the eyes when compared to my own. I will squash him and fuck the remnants of his corpse until he's nothing but a little red smear across my pronged cock. I'm full of anger, nearly bubbling with it. I'm ascending as fast as I can along the earthen walls, crawling and scraping my way up through the tunnel.

He will die slow; I'll start with the legs, I'll...what the fuck?

What is this little black speck falling towards me? I see something sharp and shiny in a tiny hand. The form is plummeting, getting closer and closer. I have a mere millisecond to see Rose. Her little eyes are very gray and very cold. They remind me of that miserable ice age.

She is slicing at me through the air. She is cutting little rivets into me. She stabs a keen blade through the gelatinous orb of one of my largest eyes and I scream in a mixture of shock and pain. This crazy little bitch is trying to blind me! I'm so surprised by the ferocity of the attack that my ascension is momentarily halted.

Finally she falls against my enormous body and I manage to desperately stab a finger upwards and skewer her with one of my fingernails. She remains impaled there on my talon, her little fishnet-clad legs kicking.

How did it all go so wrong?

Black blood and yellow pus drips down from my mangled eye. I can still only fit a portion of my body out of the hole and this was my best eye for seeing above the surface. It's blinded now, showing me nothing but murky shadows.

I resume my ascension.

I'm going to torture Roman Merrick extra slow for this.

Chapter 61

Roman

I watch Rose leap down into the pit through half-lidded eyes. Moments later the invisible hands around my throat fall away. I fall forward onto my hands and knees, coughing and sputtering for breath. I tear fresh oxygen into my chest and already I'm stumbling up to my feet and moving. I don't have much time. I grab the can of gasoline and I spill the contents down into the pit, splashing the walls as much as I can.

Having done that I race out the open door and I climb into the cage of the big PC400 excavator. I turn the key in the ignition and start the engine just as M bursts up out of the pit. He starts bashing and tearing at the weak walls around him and the root cellar is literally torn to shreds in the wake of his wrath. All that remains is the pit surrounded by splintered rubble and M's hideous segmented body emerging out of it.

The part of M that I can see turns my stomach. He's horribly pale, almost albinistic. Deep blue varicose veins cover his engorged flesh and weeping sores mar just about every inch of him. He has multitudes of questing arms that end in long, clawed fingers. There's not much of a head to be seen, just a lump of flesh that has a long slit across it. That slit opens to hundreds of sharp and yellowed teeth. They spin in the motion of a circular saw. It's like staring into the maws of a whole legion of lampreys. There are eyes all over him, blinking and wet with white ooze. The largest of these eyes appears to be mutilated and dripping with a mixture of noxious internal fluids.

A weak whisper invades my ears and I turn my head to see Thorny Rose just a few inches away from my face. Her black clothes are saturated in blood and a crusty fingernail juts out of her chest. Her little hands grip the talon that impales her. Plasma pours down past her lips and drips off her chin.

"Ro..."

181

It's just a dying croak. My heart breaks for my friend. I know she's done awful things in service of M, but I can't help but feel sorry for her. She reaches out with trembling hands and holds my cheeks.

"Just one kiss..."

She presses her bloody, quivering lips against my own. I taste her coppery blood. I taste the madness and the obsession swirling inside of her. I taste death as it comes to take her. She's immediately pulled away as M flicks his hand backwards.

Rose's torn body slides off the fingernail and tumbles down past M's segmented form and right back into the pit. She vanishes beyond M's girth. Poor, broken creature. M cranes backwards and howls at the overcast sky, his shriek shattering the entire foundation of the house. The old building crumbles and falls, ruined by the vibrations from the deep. I clamp my hands over my ears and struggle to endure.

M moves incredibly fast, his body snapping forward and one of his long fingers extending into the cage of the excavator to stab into the flesh of my shoulder. The pain is hot and immediate and the blood starts to run down past the wound.

M tries to press his mouth up against the cab of the excavator now, his teeth spinning erratically as he endeavors to devour me. A long, rough tongue snakes out to lap across my face, leaving stinking saliva across my features. I can smell so many lives rotting down in M's guts.

I reach desperately for a lever and manage to yank it to the side with my good arm. The hydraulic arm swings around and the steel bucket slams into M's segmented body and knocks him away from the cab. The fingernail exits my shoulder and fresh blood drips down. M actually falls down against the ground, his many arms trying to support his weight.

I reach down into my pocket with shivering hands and I retrieve my battered zippo. My face feels very wet and my heart is hammering. I have only one chance at this. I have to make it count. I flick the flint wheel and a tiny flame appears.

I narrow my eyes. I imagine where I want the lighter to go. My aim has to be true.

I whip my hand backwards and throw the lighter with every bit of force I can muster. It bounces off a section of M's body and then lands right across the edge of the pit. The gasoline ignites and flames burst into life all around M. The voracious one hisses in anguish and begins to flop from side to side, his arms flailing. Sections of his segmented body start to blacken and char.

M has no choice. He has to withdraw back into the pit in an effort to escape the flames. His girth slithers and pulls back down into the hole. The inferno becomes even stronger now, the old wood of the root cellar feeding it. The last image I see of M is a few long fingers descending as the flames rise higher.

I'm not done yet. I work the lever again and start to dig and scrape the steel bucket of the excavator against the soil. I fill the bucket to the max and I bring the hydraulic arm up higher, the first bucket hanging ominously overtop the pit.

I let the dirt fall into the burning abyss.

Chapter 62

M

I can smell myself burning. I am singed and raw. I'm reminded of the asteroid that fell such a very long time ago. It scorched the earth. Now I'm the one scorched. I have to descend lower and lower to snuff the flames from my body. The smoke curls all around me and I see nothing. Rose's corpse is snagged on a root and a permanent grin is fixed on her dead face as I descend down past her.

She seems to ridicule me even from the jaws of death.

This boy cannot defeat the likes of me. I am Unknowable. I've always been here and this world is just my dinner plate. I am deathless and forever. How can he overcome the eternal? His existence is nothing but a little flickering candle flame while my endless life burns with the fury of Tartarus.

I want to rise, but I'm weak and burnt and I cannot rise. Something is happening up there. Dirt is falling down against my eyes. I am being buried. I am being sealed in the deep. The passageway is being severed. I watch as the hole vanishes and the silence of my prison becomes unbearable.

There is only darkness now.

Much like myself, I think this darkness is forever.

Chapter 63

Roman

I keep filling the excavator's steel bucket full of dirt and piling it down on top of the hole over and over again. I don't stop shoveling soil down into the hole until I've made a large man-made hill where the root cellar once stood. A fitting burial mound for the thing that dwells beneath.

Finally I stop myself and scrub the sweat from my brow. Everything is quiet. The earth no longer quakes and there are no vibrations from below. My shoulder throbs but at least the blood seems to have stopped flowing for the moment.

I carefully climb down from the excavator. There's a piece of something black sticking up out of the dirt. I pull at it and unearth a heavy backpack. I take a look inside and marvel at the various precious stones contained within. I sling the backpack over my good shoulder and I take one last look at the burial mound I've created. I hope Rose finds peace in whatever lies beyond this life.

As for M?

Let him rot.

I limp my way over to the Dodge Charger and toss the backpack into the passenger seat. I slide gingerly behind the wheel and I drive away from Legion Lane just as the sun blazes into view from behind the mountains. I drive until I've passed beyond the town limits of Rust Valley and then I keep on driving.

I've never looked back.

Chapter 64

Epilogue

Three years later.

My family and I live in the Bahamas now. Helena spends her time drinking cold lemonade on white sand beaches. Her dystonia gradually abated until all symptoms vanished completely. That was one gift M never got to take back.

Braham owns a small chain of tiki bars on the islands and business is good. Money problems are a thing of the past for us. I guess M kept that promise too, whether he wanted to or not.

I take long walks when the tide comes in and I let the waters of the Atlantic wash across my ankles. I think about Rust Valley sometimes. I think about holes in the dirt and holes inside of people and the old, hungry thing that lived beneath the house on Legion Lane. I doubt he's dead. I don't think something like him can ever really die. He's buried and forgotten though, and that's good enough for me.

Rose Crimshire is still listed as missing. The only crime she was ever connected to was the suspected murder of her mother Rebecca, also missing. The case is dead in the water and no new evidence has come to light. It never will.

Any plans for a quarry to be dug on the property died with Rose. Greystone Construction took their equipment and abandoned the site shortly after learning that she lied about owning the land. There wasn't any money to keep them there either, so I'm sure that played into it. The collapse of the house was blamed on a small earthquake. Rare for that part of West Virginia, but the seismic readings couldn't be denied.

The house was bulldozed completely and demolished shortly after. I haven't been back since but I understand all that stands there now is a vacant lot surrounded by chain link fencing. There are no plans to do much of anything with the land that remains there.

I still drive the fastest 1968 Dodge Charger this world has ever known. I like to drive it down Western Road with the windows down and gaze out at the clear waters of Old Fort Bay. The radio has a mind of its own and only ever plays one song, but I've always liked Blue Oyster Cult's "Don't Fear The Reaper" so I don't mind that so much.

One evening I was driving and saw two figures standing out there on a tiny deserted island in the bay. The man was tall and handsome and his hair was slicked back from his forehead. He wore the finest brown suede suit I've ever seen. He had a little blonde girl with him in a pretty yellow dress. Her left hand was holding the man's hand and her right was holding a little bouquet of daffodils.

They waved at me as I passed. I waved back. When I looked into the rear view mirror to get another glimpse of them they were already gone.

Nights are beautiful in the Bahamas. Sometimes I sit on a pristine beach during high tide and I just stare up at the stars. They're so bright I'm often tempted to reach out and try to touch them.

I think there are holes inside of all of us, some deep, some shallow. You live and you learn and you try to fill them up as you go. Sometimes people fill them up with an idealized image of someone they crave. I think of Rose, her shy smile and a book always lying open in her lap. Sometimes people fill them with lost loved ones. I think of James and his sharp suits and his little daughter with her daffodils. Sometimes people fill them with the promise of a better life. I think of myself, venturing down into the dark with a flashlight in hand after the electric was shut off years ago.

Everyone has a void inside of them. Every void is personal and you fill it up as best you can. It's all about driving away the emptiness. You fill the void until you finally feel whole. I'm whole now. My family is whole.

We're happy.

We're free.

Chapter 65

Forgotten Holes

Spring has come to Rust Valley and new life is everywhere. The grass is green and the trees hang heavy with newborn leaves. Squirrels chatter and hunt down nuts while robins sing from power lines. Two little boys totter down Legion Lane with colorful buckets and little garden trowels in hand. It's a warm, sunny afternoon. The perfect kinda day for making mud pies.

They talk about all the popular topics boys their age like to talk about. Cartoons and comics and the next big blockbuster superhero flick coming to theaters in a few weeks. They look for the absolute best spot to make their pies. Making mud pies is serious business and only the best dirt will suffice.

They pass by the empty lot near the end of the lane and they stare through the fencing. There's a big hill in there all grown over with wildflowers. Best dirt they've seen all day! The boys are small and they easily squeeze themselves through a little tear in the fencing.

The boys climb the hill and set their buckets down next to a bloom of wild roses. They start digging and packing dirt into the buckets and patting down their pies. Suddenly one of the boys stops patting pies, his forehead wrinkling in bewilderment. He presses his ear down against the dirt.

"What you doing, doofus?"

"Hush. I hear somethin."

"What is it?"

"I dunno. It's like…singing. Sounds like a lullaby."

The other boy pushes his ear down against the dirt too, his mop of red hair flattening against the earth. He notices a little hole that seems to be the source of the sound. He can almost fit half his pinky finger into it.

"Weird. I hear somethin too."

"Wonder what's down there?"

The redhead looks at his friend and shrugs.

"Let's see."

188

The boys take up their garden trowels and start digging.

Something small and slithery crawls up onto a mossy rock to watch them. It rests beneath the shade of a willow tree and twitches many pairs of legs together. Mandibles click and stretch.

The house centipede seems almost to smile.

November 1st 2014- January 7th 2015

Jeremy Megargee

ABOUT THE AUTHOR:

When I was still a child and picked up my very first Goosebumps book by R. L. Stine, I knew I'd fallen head over heels in love with all things horror. It's a love affair that has only grown stronger over the years, a borderline obsession with stories that explore the darkest recesses of the human imagination. I guess you could say I'm like Thorny Rose in that way...always stalking down those special stories that have the ability to invoke a creepy-crawly feeling right down in the marrow of my bones.

As I grew older I discovered the work of some of my biggest inspirations like Stephen King, Edgar Allan Poe, H.P. Lovecraft, Clive Barker...and the work of those authors sent me deeper down the path of the macabre. During my teenage years I had the little tradition of reading Stephen King's The Stand each summer to lose myself in the devastation of the superflu and marvel at the sadistic magnetism of Randall Flagg.

I've devoured horror fiction for as long as I can remember and reading the words weaved by the greats of the genre inspired me to begin writing. I wanted the opportunity to tell my own tales with the intent to terrify, to disturb; to capture the morbid curiosity of the reader just as my own was caught so early on in life.

If I've managed to inspire some of those feelings in you, my readers, then I feel that I've accomplished something just a little bit magical. There's still some magic left in this world, and I think it's most powerful when manifested in the form of words scrawled across many blank pages. Granted any magic contained within my work will be of the dark variety...but I wouldn't want it any other way. ;)

I live in Martinsburg, West Virginia with my little old pug Cerberus. When I'm not writing, I enjoy hiking mountain trails, weight training, getting tattooed and being a garden variety introvert in his mid-20s. Oh, and reading too (duh).

Connect with me online:

Facebook: www.facebook.com/JMHorrorFiction

Instagram: @xbadmoonrising

FUTURE WORK:
Stay tuned for my second novel, "Sweet Treats"...release date TBA soon!

Thanks for reading!

<u>What did you think of DIRT LULLABIES?</u>

Feedback is incredibly important for indie authors. Most indie authors are not affiliated with Big Publishing and we don't have the vast resources or marketing tools to get our names out there compared to many of the advertised best-selling titles. Reviews give my work additional exposure and help new readers to discover my particular brand of horror.

If you enjoyed this book, I would love it if you could head over to the Amazon.com page for Dirt Lullabies and leave an honest review about what you thought of the story. I read every single review I get and I'm very grateful for the support.

Feel free to share this book with friends, word of mouth advertising goes a long way...and it helps the horror spread. ;)

Made in the USA
Middletown, DE
28 October 2020